## "There's something you must know, Greg."

Sara's heart began to thud in slow pounding strokes. Then Greg was saying, "No, we'll talk later, Sara."

Sara was carried away by the strength in his kiss. She didn't even struggle. *This is what I wanted all along,* she thought hazily. Something came to her then, and she struggled to be coherent. "Greg I've got to tell you," she began, but was effectively cut off by another deep, long, mind-weakening kiss.

His kiss moved down her throat, searching, caressing. He raised his head, looked into her eyes, and she knew him in that moment and then knew herself.

Greg needed her now, tonight. She opened her mouth to tell him the truth and she couldn't.

Tomorrow faded away like morning mist.

# Books by Amanda Carpenter

**HARLEQUIN PRESENTS**
703—THE WALL

**HARLEQUIN ROMANCES**
2605—A DEEPER DIMENSION

These books may be available at your local bookseller.

For a free catalog listing all titles currently available,
send your name and address to:

Harlequin Reader Service
P.O. Box 52040, Phoenix, AZ   85072-2040
Canadian address: P.O. Box 2800, Postal Station A,
5170 Yonge St., Willowdale, Ont.   M2N 5T5

# AMANDA CARPENTER

## the wall

**Harlequin Books**

TORONTO • NEW YORK • LONDON
AMSTERDAM • PARIS • SYDNEY • HAMBURG
STOCKHOLM • ATHENS • TOKYO • MILAN

Harlequin Presents first edition July 1984
ISBN 0-373-10703-X

Original hardcover edition published in 1984
by Mills & Boon Limited

# CHAPTER ONE

SARA was tired of the house, having spent so much time inside lately to arrange the furniture and various other things to her liking, and so she took one look at the fine sunny morning outside on the early October Monday, and decided to take a walk.

She had just spent a long moment in the bathroom, looking at herself in the mirror, and she hadn't liked what she had seen. She hadn't noticed the glossy black hair that swirled off of her fine forehead to tumble down her shoulders in a cloudy darkness, nor had she particularly paid much attention to the clear quality of her smooth white complexion. She spared only the most cursory of glances for her large hazel eyes that seemed a different colour with every different colour of clothing that she wore. At the moment, her eyes were a deep blue flecked with just a hint of green around the pupil, reflecting the shade of her pullover sweater. They were fringed with long brown lashes that curled slightly on the ends.

She had been busy looking at the tiny wrinkles that radiated from the corner of her eyes to spread like a nearly invisible fan out to the temples. She had taken great care in inspecting the small creases that accompanied her rather generous mouth, one line to each side. To be entirely truthful, one could not see those lines on her face unless one were to peer at the skin from the distance of about three inches (a distance that made her feel like going cross-eyed in the bathroom mirror), but she knew they were there, and suddenly on that quiet Monday morning the knowledge made her feel every one of her twenty-eight years. She didn't like the feeling. Her energy flow was at low tide at the moment, and this combined with the fear of getting old was a bit much to handle on a Monday.

And so, with a hunted look at the wonderful bright day that had just recently begun, she decided to take that walk. This freedom to take off outside whenever she wanted to was just the sort of thing that she had dreamed about for months. It was for this freedom that she had spent months in a veritable whirlwind of activity, rearranging her work schedule and setting a bruising pace for the final effort on the cutting of her latest music album. She had pushed too hard, perhaps, and it showed in little ways: the slight shake to her hands, the thinness of her figure, the increase of her cigarette smoking to almost two packs a day. Whether the extra strain had been worth it or not, she couldn't yet say. She was conscious only of a very great tiredness, and an immense relief that the album was at last behind her and the contract completed. Now she had nothing to look forward to except for the empty autumn days that stretched ahead of her, tantalising and free.

No one knew where she was, and that was probably the factor that made everything so enjoyable. Barry, her agent, hadn't a clue, and in spite of all his protestations and expostulations, she had kept it that way. As she let herself out of her small rented cabin, she hugged the coffee thermos and knapsack to her side with glee. Who in their right mind would guess that Sara Bertelli, one of the brightest and most popular modern singers to hit the top of nationwide music charts, would be tramping about on the shores of Lake Michigan and living just north of an obscure little one-stop-light town named Three Oaks? She flattered herself to think that no one would, and took a great deal of effort to congratulate herself on just that. It had been a good idea, staying not twenty miles away from her home town. It symbolised a trip back to the roots of her personality, which was what she was doing, searching herself and going back to the basics. Her real name was Sara Carmichael, and some deeply rooted instinct, only half conscious, kept her from revealing her true name and birthplace to anyone outside of Barry and his wife Elise. It was something she had considered too private; perhaps something inside her had foreseen the need to get away for a while. She didn't know.

It had been years since she had been to Michigan, and she had lost contact with the few friends that she had once had as everyone gradually moved away to different cities. For all practical purposes, she was a virtual stranger to the area.

She had rented the cabin under her real name, and had taken care that few people should see her well-known face. Not, she told herself, that anyone would be likely to recognise her. Without the heavy and dramatic make-up that she affected for album covers, photographs and public appearances, she looked almost ordinary. One might look twice and then again one might not, whereas in her professional guise one always looked again. The press went wild over her face, for with the dramatic make-up she looked like a temptress, with a sultry, brooding dark beauty that stared into the camera's eye with a half sullen, half seductive look. The one part of her that didn't change when she was not in the public eye was the lustrous, shining quality to her heavy black hair. It was wholly natural, a throwback to several generations earlier in her genealogy when an immigrant Italian beauty had married into the Carmichael family. It was her true claim to beauty.

Sara shook the mass of darkness away from her face now without a single thought for its thick vitality, and stepped down the beckoning footpath that led practically up to her back door. She surmised that it should lead her straight to the lake, judging by the direction it was heading, and as this was her goal she decided to see where the path went.

The beach was very easy to find. The path was rather straight to the point, and after about five minutes Sara caught a whiff of something cool and fresh on the carrying breeze, and her head raised like that of a scenting hound's, her fine nostrils widening and her eyes searching. Then as she rounded a bend in the path, she saw a patch of blue. Soon the hard-packed earth underneath her feet became loose and shifty and the treeline broke open to harsh grasses rising from rippling dunes. She rounded yet another bend in the path and found herself out on an open beach with a deep blue expanse that travelled as far as the eye could see.

The sound of the waves hitting the shore, the overhead cry of birds, and the incredible fresh quality to the breeze that hit her so gently made her close her eyes for a moment and sigh deeply in appreciation and contentment. She walked out of the protection of the trees and towards the water. Away from the obstruction of the treeline, she took stock of the shoreline from both the northern direction and the southern, resting her knapsack and camera bag at her feet as she surveyed the area with a hand shading her eyes from the noon sun. To the south, which was left of her, off in the misty blue distance she saw the Cook's nuclear power plant at the edge of the water, and farther from that several small bright patches of colour that proclaimed late season swimmers taking advantage of the unusually warm weather. To the right she saw some distance to a rather high jutting shoreline that dropped some thirty feet into the water and effectively cut the other side off from her sight. It was sufficiently intriguing for her to set off in that direction, her small knapsack and camera bag bumping her knee as she trod along.

Photography had been an interest of hers for years,

and now she fully intended to take the time to indulge her hobby. She wanted to get some pictures of the shoreline, and to possibly come back that evening to shoot the sunset on the waters of Lake Michigan. Sara climbed the rise in the shoreline and stood at the top of the small cliff. She stared down at the other side, disappointed. Just at the bottom of the rise, 'No Trespassing' signs were posted. After staring at the sign for some minutes and thinking of the people sure to be populating the beach in the other direction, she made up her mind. Chances were that the person who owned the property wouldn't catch her just this once on the land, and the barren sight of the empty expanse that stretched ahead was just too much to resist. She climbed down the other side of the cliff and continued the way she had originally headed. After a time, revelling in the seclusion of the sandy beach—and knowing full well that a large measure of her enjoyment was derived from the forbidden nature of her jaunt—Sara had an attractive idea. She slid her burden down to the ground and after rolling up her jeans, dropped to her knees in the sand and started to scoop up handfuls in a decisive way. Soon she was engrossed in the makings of a fine sand castle, so reminiscent of the ones from her childhood. She stopped once to look around for a few pieces of wood and a couple of sticks to dig with, and she soon had a deep hole with high, even sides all around. As she worked, the golden sun and fresh air, the interminable sound of lapping waves and incessant cry of wild birds, the pervading quiet under all of the surface sounds, all made her gradually relax. The tension in her neck and shoulder muscles melted away. Her lips began to smile slightly as the wind whipped her dark hair around her neck and into her eyes. She earnestly started on taking out regular block chunks from the top of the wall to make a credible rampart, when a shadow fell across her handiwork.

To the man watching, Sara seemed to be no bigger than a child crouching at play. Her slender legs shone white in the afternoon sunlight and delicate blue veins wove a tapestry in her small feet. Her long thin fingers moved rapidly and gracefully, the blue veins apparent also on the back of her hands. The dark hair was tangled on her neck.

She stared at the square shadow in front of her with some amusement before addressing it. 'You're probably the owner, aren't you, or someone vastly important like the sole caretaker in complete charge and authority?' she asked calmly. 'Now you've spoiled the fun. You were supposed to find my mysterious footprints and a splendid sand castle erected to guard the empty expanse of land from the mischevous and malicious water nymphs who steal babies and pick all the wild flowers ...' Just at that moment, a section of her castle wall began to cave in towards the hole, and she scrabbled over frantically. 'Yipe! Oh—shoot, it took me forever to get it right, and I haven't a picture of it yet ... oh, thanks!' This last was said as, after an apparent hesitation, the large shadow dropped beside her and two large and deeply tanned hands came alongside hers to firmly press the crumbling sand into place.

A low, pleasantly smooth voice with a curiously hard undertone reached her ears. 'I suppose you've decided to be hanged as much for a sheep as for a lamb?'

She relaxed slightly, hands hovering overhead as she backed up from the defective wall a little, refraining from looking at the man by her side. What kind of face would go with a voice like that? she wondered in a pleasantly idle speculation. 'Something like that,' she laughed softly, the sound of it coming from her throat like a rich purr. She picked up her stick and started again on the uniform blocks on the top of the wall with a great deal of care and precision. 'My mother always told me I should have been an engineer. I was forever building things with my blocks and playing with the neighbour boy's construction set instead of with my dolls.' When she had things to her satisfaction, she slid back in the sand to look at it thoughtfully. Then she turned with a smile to face the stranger. 'But I'm sure you don't want to hear about me.'

His gaze was not directed towards the sand castle but was shot piercingly at her. She let her own mild gaze roam over hard, irregular features set in what she took to be a very bitter expression. Sitting back on her heels, she took more time to assess this unknown person. Her first impression held; lines running down the sides of the man's mouth were scored deeply, and the firm mouth was held in a way that seemed to be at once stern and unhappy. The eyes that were watching her so speculatively were a dark brown, and they were the hardest eyes that she had ever seen. They hid something inside, repelling her scrutiny like a brick wall. The man appeared to be bulky, but his heavy sweater and jeans as he squatted on his heels might account for that. As she watched him, a light breeze stirred his dark hair into his eyes and a shapely, strong-looking hand swept it back impatiently.

The mutual perusal took a few moments for each of them. Neither had spoken since she had. The strange man was still watching her, and she smiled again at him suddenly, the white flash of her teeth brilliant and surprising. 'Do you have a Kleenex, or a handkerchief, or something like that?' she asked him conversationally, digging into her own jeans pocket as she talked. 'No, forget it, thanks. I've got a folded Kleenex.' She shook it out carefully, took the slender stick that had once served as her digging tool and gently poked the stick through several times, back and forth, through the end of the tissue. Then she stuck it gingerly at the top of the wall. The wall deigned to hold up. 'What's the forfeit for a picture?'

A glance at him found the man strangely tense, watching her with a harsh, mocking light in his eyes that uncomfortably reminded her of a bird of prey watching its victim. 'It depends on what you plan on taking a picture of,' was his silky reply, and she stared at him in confoundment.

Her reply was snappy, since she hadn't liked the tone of his voice. 'You couldn't suppose me to want a picture of you, could you? Heavens, you don't look a bit photogenic—would you mind stepping back so I can get a clear shot of my castle?' She reached for her camera bag and dug out her Minolta, looking at his still outline as he stood in the sun. 'Look, you have every earthly right to throw me off your land, but I want a picture of this castle. It took me ages to finish, and I'm going to get a picture of it whether you move or not.' She added with a touch of childish petulance that was not wholly put on, as she took off the camera lens cover, 'You'll very likely ruin the shot, too, glowering at me like that!'

At this muttered remark, surprisingly, the man threw back his head and laughed. He stepped back a few paces to stand with hands resting lightly on hips, and she eyed him with approval. 'You aren't half bad when you aren't glowering,' she told him mildly, and turned to focus experimentally on the sand castle. After a second, she clicked the shutter with satisfaction. Then she sat back on her heels to survey the stranger's tense stance. She reached into her knapsack, still watching the man, and was rewarded with a close, wary scrutiny. What in the world, she wondered curiously, is that man so jumpy about? She held out her pack of cigarettes to him invitingly, but he shook his head in silent refusal. She shrugged, took one herself, and lit up expertly.

'How did you get to this beach?' the man asked her, dropping down on the sand nearby and still favouring her with his unsettling gaze. It was the look of an opponent sizing up the enemy, she thought, but shrugged away the thought with an involuntary grimace. The man sat easily, knees drawn up and arms draped casually on top, with hands loosely laced. His harsh face was expressionless, and again Sara got the strange impression that he was erecting a wall between himself and her. It was not as if she were anyone especially threatening to him, she realised, and she surmised that it must be a characteristic that he exhibited to all strangers. That was perfectly understandable to her. She had learned to be wary of strangers herself. She drew hard on her cigarette, and expelled the smoke appreciatively, and then pointed to the southern shoreline. He spared a brief glance for the direction of her gesture and then returned his keen gaze to her face. 'That's private property too.'

She nodded, regarding him with a faint smile. 'I'm one of your neighbours, temporarily at least. I've a six-month lease on the cabin that probably sits adjacent to your south border. It's a small place, one car garage, archaic plumbing and two fireplaces with no firewood! Know of it?'

He nodded in reply, the action making his hair tousle in the breeze. She spared some time appreciating the red glints in the brown hair—hers was so dark there was no doubt that it was one shade only, namely, black as midnight—and then noticed just how closely he was watching her. It was getting on her nerves. 'I wasn't aware that anyone was living there,' was his only response, though.

'I've been there only about a week,' she told him, 'so I'm fairly new around here.' She put out her cigarette by burying the glowing tip in the sand. Aware of the dark gaze on her actions, she took the dead butt and carefully wrapped it in the castle's banner before stuffing it into the knapsack. Then, nervous for some reason, she took another and lit up to inhale it in deeply.

After a moment, he asked almost idly, 'Are you in the habit of trespassing on private property?'

'Wince!' she said, and laughed at his expression. She leaned back casually in the soft, inviting sand. 'Now the retribution, please show mercy on my poor soul. If I'm missing for more than three years or so, or get behind in my rent, someone may just miss me and become suspicious, so don't do anything rash, will you? ... Actually, a 'No Trespassing' sign is so inviting, don't you think? I came, entertaining half acknowledged hopes of stumbling on to a dead body and a delightfully chilling mystery, or perhaps to meet up with a terrible ogre—are you an ogre?' This last was said with a hopeful glance towards the man's uncompromising face.

No sign of amusement there, the face was settled into lines of implacable hardness, the eyes like stones. The one sign that perhaps redeemed his face, she thought musingly, was the unhappy curve to that well formed mouth. She watched him with a great deal of interest. His reply was brief, almost a snap. 'Some seem to think so.'

A chuckle bubbled forth. 'Well, are they right or are they wrong?' He only looked at her with dark, expressionless eyes, and it seemed so terrible to her that she, on impulse, had made an uncharacteristic gesture of friendliness to the man. She finished her cigarette, condemned the butt to a similar fate as the first and asked him, 'Would I get perhaps fewer lashes of the whip if I were to bribe my punisher with a cup of coffee?'

He hesitated, obviously, and she thought he was about to refuse when he said carefully, 'It depends on what terrible things you've doctored your thermos of coffee with.'

Sara smiled involuntarily, tossing her dark hair off from her face, and it settled around her shoulders like a smoky cloud. 'Not me, mister. I like my mud straight.'

She poured him a cup of the warm liquid into a plastic cup that she had packed and handed it to him cordially, taking her own in the lid of the thermos. He took it after eyeing her with those curiously hard brown eyes.

She stared off into the distance, appreciating the smoky blue horizon and sipping her coffee reflectively. She was a bit puzzled as to why she should make such uncharacteristic overtures to a total stranger. She wasn't sure why. It could be reaction, she surmised, a touch of cabin fever, having been off on her own for a week. It could be an attempt to break the mould she had become frozen into after so many years. She had always surrounded herself in a shell of aloofness when greeting strangers, for she had learned to be wary of reporters and curiosity seekers, it was a wall not unlike the almost visible one surrounding the stranger sitting close to her. In a way, she mused, we all build walls around ourselves for one reason or another. Fear of failure, rejection, hurt, all these were reasons why one would close oneself off from other people. Everyone, to some extent, hid behind a wall. It was just a matter of how high and how strong one built it.

She rather thought that the look of bitterness and unhappiness that was betrayed in the way the man held his firm mouth was the reason she impulsively reached out to him, in spite of the hard and repelling quality to his eyes. She inspected his face. He was sipping at the hot liquid and staring into the water.

They sat thus in a strangely companionable silence for several minutes, Sara filling up the cups with more coffee when they both had finished the first. Then she dug into her knapsack and presented the man with an apple, which he took gravely. She took one herself and chomped reflectively.

'You know,' she said around a bite, 'you aren't as bad as you first seemed. I was sure you were going to have me arrested. You aren't even bad-looking and would probably photograph all right, so I'm sorry for what I said earlier.' Her hazel eyes danced. 'I don't go in for photographing people, that's all.'

He told her implacably, 'I don't go in for being photographed, so you're safe from insulting me. And I'm not exactly pretty material.'

'No,' she said, studying his features, 'pretty is not how I would describe you. You've more of a presence than a profile. Want a sandwich?'

'Won't I be taking your meal?'

'Lord, no—I've got two.' A sandwich passed hands as gravely as the apple had. This time he murmured a thanks, and the two sandwiches quickly went the way of the apples, disappearing fast, and in the same companionable silence. Sara took a long look at the man beside her. 'I can't figure out why you haven't kicked me off of the property yet,' she told him matter-of-factly.

A swift turn of the head, and she saw again those hard, watching eyes. She must have been mistaken about that silence being companionable. 'I've been thinking about just who you could be and why you're here. I haven't come to any conclusions, so why don't you tell me who you are?'

Nice, tactful question, that, she thought. 'Who I am doesn't really matter,' was her calm reply, though she was hiding an underlying uneasiness. He couldn't have recognised her, could he? The beach was very, very empty, and she noticed it suddenly. 'But, if you would like to have a name to attach to a face, my name is Sara Carmichael. I've been ill and this is my recuperation,' and she swung out a flamboyant hand that encompassed the entire scene. 'My parents are dead, I'm unmarried, no close relatives. Life is rather dull at the moment, but I'm liking it that way for a change. I'm twenty-eight years old, and have suddenly realised that my thirty-year milestone mark is breathing down my neck, and it has me slightly panicked at the thought, and that's about it.'

'In a nutshell,' he murmured, and she had to chuckle.

'Sad in a way, isn't it? An entire human life and thinking awareness can be described so simply and dully.' She took out another cigarette and lit it. Her hand, she noticed absently, was shaking less now. Soon she would be back to normal. But what was normal, any more? 'I could walk out in that water right now, and not come back, and no one would really miss me.' She caught his complete stillness and shocked eyes and had to laugh. 'Don't worry, I am *not* contemplating suicide! I'm merely expressing how total the waste of a life can be. I should know, I've wasted twenty-eight years, and I'll never get them back again. It's only now that I've begun to suspect that I've never really lived.'

Strange, she thought in a detached way, how comforting it is to talk about oneself with a stranger. It was a good feeling, rather like what a Catholic would feel after making a confession to a priest behind a curtain. This man didn't know her and probably never would. She could say the most truthful and outrageous things she wanted to and feel sure he would never know who she really was and what she was talking about.

A sudden comment made her start in surprise. 'You smoke too much for an invalid,' the man told her expressionlessly. 'In fact, you smoke too much for a healthy individual.'

Sara looked up with a kind of shocked feeling, meeting dark and almost blank eyes. Almost. Deep down there was a flicker of—interest? Of concern? No, not that, she was a stranger and meant nothing to him . . . whatever it was, it dispelled the hard and implacable quality that she had first seen in his eyes. A slow smile spread over her face and it was like a ray of sunshine. She looked at the smoking cigarette in her hand as if she had never seen it before, then stubbed it out.

'You see?' she said. 'A total waste of life so far. You're absolutely right! And I'll tell you this right now: I quit. How does that sound? Only I hope I can do it, I've never tried to quit smoking before, you know, and I smoke a lot. Well, if one is determined and all, etcetera, and so on.'

'Eloquently put,' he drawled, looking for a moment amused. Sara grinned amiably, glad to see a lighter expression on his face. She was sprawled all over the sand, the rolled-up jeans revealing slim ease, and she absently reached down to dust off her feet. Her hair lifted off her neck in a puff of wind, and she reached up with a long-fingered thin hand to straighten it, looking over the water with a peaceful feeling. It showed in her eyes, and her lips were turned up at the corner ever so slightly. The man's head was turned her way.

'Shall I apologise?' she asked, without looking away from the water.

'For what?'

'Trespassing, silly. If I apologise nicely, will it get me off the hook?' She turned at that and looked at him mournfully, her big eyes soulful and solemn. 'I truly am sorry.'

He regarded her, and a faint smile touched the edges of his lips, banishing the unhappy look, 'No, you're not.'

'Well,' she returned, 'it sounded good, didn't it?'

At that he really did laugh, and the sound was rich and glad. She felt absurdly happy hearing it; when she had first seen him she had wondered if he ever laughed at all. After watching him with appreciation, she began to gather up her things. He told her, 'You're absolved of all crime.'

'How nice.' Dusting off her feet as best she could, she started to put on her socks and shoes and thought better of it, tying them to the knapsack instead. She picked up her camera bag and would have put that on her shoulder too, but was stopped when a big hand took it from her and took her knapsack too. She stared at the man in surprise.

'I'll carry them for you,' he said easily, slinging them on his own broad shoulder. Sara regarded him with a faint twinkle in her eyes.

'Do I have a choice?' she asked the world in general. Then she addressed him personally. 'You really don't have to feel compelled to show me off the property. I promise to leave!'

'It's my pleasure,' he murmured, looking down at her from his superior height. This rankled. He was a stranger and had no reason to feel favourably inclined towards her, but to say such a thing after just spending an agreeable hour in her company was a bit of an insult.

'I suppose,' she said a little stiffly, 'I should thank you.'

'Not at all.' They climbed the rise and slid down the other side. He moved quickly and easily in the sand, and she was soon hard put to it to keep up with his longer stride. Finally she had to beg him to slow down, which he did immediately, waiting for her to catch up. She drew up alongside him, inwardly angry at him for his apparent eagerness to get rid of her and furious at herself for feeling angry at him. It shouldn't matter one way or the other.

When they had reached the path that led to her back door, he handed her the bags and stepped out of the way so that she could pass. She nodded pleasantly to him, determined to be polite and uncaring, then stopped to gape at his words when he told her quietly, 'Feel free to come exploring on the beach whenever you like.'

She stared and then managed to reply, 'Are you sure? I mean, I don't want to be an imposition on your privacy.'

He looked down at her with an enigmatic look, eyes taking in every detail. 'I'm sure. You'll be welcome.'

She was silent for a minute at this. 'Would it be all right if I came back this evening to take a picture of the sunset? You really don't mind me tramping about on the beach?'

'I really don't mind, and yes, feel free to come whenever you like. The house is well back from the beach, so you won't be invading my privacy.'

Nice hint, that, she thought. 'Very well, if you're sure, then.' A thought struck her and she laughed. 'What do I call you, anyway?'

He was standing with hands pushed into his jeans pockets, the stance hunching his shoulders, and his feet were planted well apart. She had a quick impression of immovable strength, and then he was moving, back up, starting to turn away. 'My name is Greg.'

She backed up herself. 'Nice meeting you, then, Greg. Thank you for letting me come back.'

'You're welcome, Sara.'

Without a backward glance, she took off up the path and soon let herself into her back door, unaware of the tall figure that stopped and turned, watching her go with unreadable eyes, following her until she was out of sight.

Back inside, Sara went about the actions of putting the knapsack away and washing her thermos and plastic cup mechanically. She spent a good deal of energy in thinking about the stranger whom she had apparently befriended. Or had she befriended him after all? He had seemed such a strange mixture of politeness and bitterness, of wariness and friendliness, of cynicism and real concern. Thinking of the man and the aura of watchful reserve that clung to him, she started to wonder at her own overtures again.

It was definitely a strange situation, for she hardly ever made casual acquaintances. But that look in the man's eyes and the unhappy nerve to his mouth had struck a spark of understanding and empathy within her. She knew how it felt to be unhappy; she had been extremely unhappy herself until just recently. She knew how it felt to be bitter and disillusioned. Perhaps that was the reason she had made such obvious overtures of friendliness. She had felt a desire to show him that there was the possibility to overcome bitterness, and to be happy after disappointment. Perhaps that was why she had spilled so much of herself out to him.

She shrugged and put the matter out of her mind for the time being. She didn't even know what prompted that strange and unhappy expression and the chances were that she never would. There was no reason for the man to wish to confide in a total stranger. She didn't even want him to, anyway.

Feeling in need of an outlet for her strangely aroused emotions, she went into the rather small living room and sat down at the ancient piano that she had just recently had tuned. Flexing her long strong fingers over the black and white keys, she emptied her mind of all thought and concentrated on the mood of the moment. Then she let her fingers come down on the keys and began to play. Strangely enough, to her mind, what she had impulsively decided to play was a sad, haunting love song that left her with unexplained tears in her eyes and an ache in her throat. She played it through several times, humming once, and then singing it softly. It left her feeling very empty.

She didn't understand it; she had never felt so lonely in her life. Suddenly, and with great impact, the realisation that she had no true friends hit her. There was no one with whom she could just be herself and not the singing star Sara Bertelli. She slowly laid her head down on the piano keyboard, her eyes shut tight. A drop eased out from the squeezed eyelids and dripped on to ivory, and then another followed.

How had she got to be twenty-eight years old without ever having a serious relationship? How could she let herself get so isolated from other human beings? Why did she let things get so hectic and unfulfilling? Why had she let ambition rule her life?

Looking back over the years, it was easy to see the progression of events. She had worked like a dog for so long, taking as many music and singing lessons as she could afford, working at nights, searching for a lucky break into the competitive field of popular music. Her talent was dynamic and did not go overlooked for long. But then there were the long, hard years of pure, intense, furious creative work. Ambition is a drug that one gets hooked on, and Sara had been a complete slave to its demands. She gave totally, with great drive and power, whether she was in the recording studio or on the stage, and the greedy public sucked it all up like a sponge taking in water. One thing led to another, until all the aspects of her life seemed to have culminated in the one event that had made her decide to leave Los Angeles for an extended, long-overdue vacation.

It had been a long day in the recording studio. The musicians were tired and irritable, and Sara's throat had ached. So had her head. She was exhausted, she remembered ruefully, and the tension of the weeks before, the terrible glittering, empty party that she had been obliged to attend the night before, and her own stretched nerves had caused her self-control to snap and she had ended up in a bitter fight with Barry, her agent. She had rushed out of the room and he had followed closely behind. Crazy, weak, infuriating tears coursed down her cheeks.

'Here, love,' Barry coaxed softly, shocked at the sight of her tired weeping, 'I know you've had a hectic time of it. We'll take a ten-minute break and get everyone a cup of coffee and into a better mood before we go on.'

She asked him, 'Couldn't we just stop for the day, Barry? I've had a total of three hours' sleep last night because of that stupid party you got me committed to going to, and an average of four or five for the past three weeks. This pace is going to kill me! Can't we slow down a little?'

'Now, baby, you know we can't, not today!' he had replied, a great deal alarmed at her show of weakness. She had never cried before, at least not that he had known of, and he didn't know how to handle a woman's tears. 'We're way behind schedule as it is, and I've got people panting down my neck for the release of this new album. I know it's a bruising pace, but it's only for another month, and then you can take a vacation. How does that sound?'

'I need a vacation now, not a month from now,' she whispered, leaning tiredly against the wall. 'Barry, I don't think I'm going to make it.'

'You will, love,' he said bracingly. Then, with more anxiety at the sad little shake of her head, he said, 'You've got to, Sara. You're committed to, by contract. You are going to make a million easily off of this album, and if you break the contract's terms by discontinuing the recording now, the studio could sue. They could ruin you financially.'

'What if they've already ruined me—if I've already ruined myself?' she had asked, unable to keep the bitterness inside.

Barry watched her closely, then reached into his pocket to draw out a small pillbox. He opened it up and held it out to her. 'Here, take one of these, love. It'll make you feel better, and then you can crash tonight. Go on, it won't hurt you.'

Tired beyond naming, depressed, discouraged and disheartened, Sara had stared at the little pillbox in Barry's hand. In her mind's eye she could see her own hand reaching out to accept what he was offering. She wanted to take that pill. She had always known that a good deal of Barry's nervous energy had come from pills in the past, but she had never questioned his personal lifestyle and he had never given her reason to fire him, for he knew his job and performed like a pure professional. She had never had any personal experience with drugs; she had always relied on her own stamina and strength.

This was what had scared her so badly, scared her into running half a continent to southern Michigan. In that one moment, she had realised just how badly she was damaging herself with her ambition and drive. She had always been determined before to keep her body free from drugs, never to develop a reliance on any type of drug. She had wanted to make her success totally on her own.

At that moment Sara realised how she had used herself. In an effort to cut an average of four albums a year and to stay at the top of the popular charts, she had sacrificed her time, energy and eventually, in the end, her self-respect. She became marketable, squelching any desire she might have felt inside to break out of the stereotype and adopt a quieter, more relaxed style of music. She had assumed an outrageous style of dress, had gone to the parties with the rich and the well-known, and had been so caught up in her own whirlwind, her personal crazy merry-go-round, that she hadn't realised just exactly when she had left her own personality behind.

The one moment, staring at a little white pill, had brought her to her senses after eight long, climbing, striving years. Sara Bertelli was a smashing success. Sara Carmichael was tired, and a little ashamed, and totally alone.

She would have to reach out to someone, before it became too late.

Thinking of this made her think of the light promise she had made to a virtual stranger that morning on the beach. She moved, with a sudden eager urgency, and took her new carton of cigarettes along with the several packs that were scattered throughout the cabin and threw them all into the cold and empty fireplace. She struck a match, watched the little flame take the end of the cardboard box and stepped back to watch the cigarettes burn away. The aromatic smell filled the room and she sniffed appreciatively. Still, she couldn't regret her actions, and a peace that was beginning to become familiar to her took her mind like a wave washing gently on a beach, and a slight smile curved her lips.

The cigarettes fell to ashes in the fireplace.

# CHAPTER TWO

Sara decided early in the evening to take another walk. She told herself that she merely wanted to get a shot of her sand castle in the sunset as she went about gathering up her camera bag and a sweater, but she knew that she wasn't being entirely truthful. There was a deeper reason, but she didn't try to dig into it. She wasn't sure that she wanted to know; it was just that suddenly the cabin seemed too small and too empty.

She swung the bag to her shoulder and headed down the path after locking her back door and slipping the key into her front jeans pocket. The path was already becoming familiar to her, and she watched for little landmarks along the way. There just ahead was a small tree that had four big bumps on its trunk, and just ahead of that was the oak tree that looked as if it had been split in two by lightning several years ago. It was still alive, and ivy tangled all over it, half hiding the scar. An elm tree to the left, a group of more oaks, and a funny little hitch in the path caused by several tangled tree roots, and then sand. A turn to the left and a patch of blue and a blaze of gold and orange from the setting sun, and she stopped to take a picture of the vivid scene before moving on.

As she climbed up the rise to reach the beach beyond, she finally admitted to herself that she had some hopes of seeing that man Greg again. For some strange reason she wanted to tell him that she burned her cigarettes. For some strange reason she hoped to make his sombre dark face smile. This admission was uncomfortable to her. She knew that now she had admitted this to herself she was going to have problems acting normally in front of him if she did run into him.

She slid down the other side of the rise, inwardly disappointed to find the sandy expanse empty. Attempting to shrug this away, she briskly took off to the sand castle, only to find it half mauled by big paw prints. Not half as disappointed at this as she was by the sight of the empty beach, Sara studied the remaining erect wall thoughtfully and decided that the ruins would look wonderful when sighted and aligned up with the setting sun. She immediately stretched out in the sand and shot the dark crumbling shape against the blazing orange orb with the haze of surrounding red, and felt well pleased.

A panting sound came to her ears and the gallop of muted feet. Thus warned, Sara attempted to roll over with the intent of rising to her feet, not wanting to be caught in such a vulnerable position. Before she could attempt to gain even her knees, a large dark shape walloped down on top of her stomach. There was a ferocious grin, a pink lolling tongue and the gleam of wicked white teeth, the pricking of interested ears, and Sara decided to remain lying down as she stared into the bright dark eyes of a very heavy Dobermann Pinscher.

She murmured gently, 'What a big boy you are! Sweetheart, good puppy. Are you always so friendly? I hope this is being friendly—I'd hate to see you unfriendly! Such a pretty puppy! Will you let me scratch your ears? Hmm?' Thus adjured, the large, extremely heavy monster sniffed inquiringly. Sara put up a very slow and careful hand, trying not to think of the sharp teeth just in front of her face, and gently scratched behind the dog's ear.

She was rewarded with a wag from the dog's stump of a tail and an appreciative whine. Feeling a little braver and very foolish, she tried stroking the sleek black head while still murmuring sweet nonsensical phrases to the grinning brute. The dog heaved a gusty sigh, put his nose to her shirt to blow noisily, and rolled over to his side, which sent him falling off of her chest. She was extremely grateful at this and managed to sit up in time to avoid having sand thrown on her face by the dog's sudden scrabbling about as he scratched his back ecstatically on the sand. This was watched with some amusement, then Sara whirled about with a start as a deep voice sounded behind her. The dog shook himself energetically and pranced over to the man to sit in front of him with an air of expectation.

'I see you've managed to run into Beowulf,' Greg commented mildly, taking in the clinging sand on her sweater and the indentations in the sand underneath her crouching body.

Feeling at a loss and quite overwhelmed by his unexpected appearance, Sara climbed to her feet slowly, brushing herself off as she murmured, 'Beowulf is quite a distinguished name, and so appropriate. Is he always so boisterous?'

'Invariably. I once entertained the hope that he would settle down when he reached adulthood, but was doomed to disappointment. He didn't get milder, only larger.' Even standing she seemed to have forgotten just how big the man was, and she stared up at him, unable to dispel a feeling of shyness. Greg looked as powerful as the heaving, panting, grinning brute at his feet. She jumped when he moved to her, saying, 'Here, let me brush off your back for you. Did he hurt you?'

'No,' she replied with a hint of self-mockery, 'only scared me a bit. Had I known that he was such a friendly dog, I wouldn't have been so ridiculously frightened. It's just when he sat on my chest and showed me those long white teeth that I——'

'Beowulf is not, I might warn, always so friendly,' he interrupted mildly as he took care to brush off her jeans too, holding her in place with one large hand to her shoulder for support. She felt like a little girl being administered to by her father. 'He had a romp this way in the afternoon, and I took care that he sniffed around at the sand castle to get used to your scent. If you'd come on to the beach and he hadn't been familiarised with you, he might have attacked.'

Sara swallowed hard. 'Oh.' His hand was brushing off the back of her thighs and she wriggled. 'I think that's good enough, thank you. Will—do you think Beowulf might bite me now?' This last was asked in a slightly anxious tone as she shot an apprehensive glance at the black, silent dog who panted calmly as he sat not five feet away.

Greg raised his head to look briefly at the dog. 'I don't think so,' he said casually. 'He didn't bite you before.'

'You don't *think* so?' she returned sarcastically. 'By the way, did I ever thank you for your generous offer to let me roam your beach freely, unaware of the dog?'

A soft chuckle sounded at this, and Greg clicked his hand at Beowulf imperatively, at which the dog immediately heaved up and advanced on the two with the most amiable of ambles.

Sara backed up sharply at this and a long hard arm snaked out to curve around her waist and pull her up short. She started to lean against it, then to wriggle protestingly as the dog came closer. 'Stop that, for heaven's sake!' Greg told her impatiently, looking down at her large eyes and apprehensive look. Then his own face softened slightly, although she was too busy noticing the dog to see it, and his voice softened too. 'Don't you see that he won't hurt you if he knows I approve of you and show you friendliness? Hold still and let him get close.'

She tried to stand calmly at this reasonable tone of voice, but couldn't help leaning back on his arm a bit as Greg moved to the dog and started to talk quietly to the beast, patting him on the head and motioning for him to come up to Sara. She stiffened as the great head lowered to her legs and feet to sniff in a totally friendly manner, and she held her breath. Beowulf snuffled about, raised his head, and wagged his stump slightly. At this, Greg told her with amusement in his voice, 'Pet him now, he won't bite. And you can let out your breath now, too.'

She expelled gustily, annoyed with his perception, and held out a tentative hand to the dog. A pink tongue lolloped her forefinger. She patted the dark head with a little more confidence and was rewarded with a happy push of the head against her legs and an adoring ogle from those velvet eyes. 'I think he likes me,' she said, delighted.

'Of course he does,' was the calm reply. She looked up as Greg told her, 'I told him he could.'

'Do you mean to tell me he's a guard dog who attacks anyone not strictly acquainted with his master?' she asked incredulously.

'Something like that,' he replied shortly. Looking down at her spilled camera bag, he asked her, 'Did you manage to get a picture of the castle ruins before Beowulf mauled you?'

'Yes. That's why I was down on the sand,' she explained, moving to pick up the things and dust them off carefully.

'I thought he'd knocked you down.'

'He probably would have if I hadn't been prone already,' she muttered, feeling annoyed when he laughed softly at that. How could she have ever wanted to hear him laugh again? It was most provoking. She stared at him consideringly, taking in the change of clothes, the nicer slacks instead of jeans and the dark sweater over a lighter shirt that was open at his strong brown throat. He looked good, and letting her eyes roam over the rather craggy features, she wondered at ever thinking him unhandsome. He was in his own way very good-looking. His dark hair was long at the back, curling over the collar of his shirt with a slight wave, and was shorter around the ears and forehead. It swept back with a natural curl. Sara averted her eyes.

His dark eyes had been trained on her and he had seen her turn away hastily. What must he think of me? she asked silently, questioning her own reaction. In those eyes she had seen for a few minutes a friendly gleam that had dispelled the hard quality from the afternoon. He had laughed, too, and although it had provoked her, she had to acknowledge that the sound had been good. With that laughter, a smile had curved the corners of his well shaped lips, and it had not been a cynical twist but a genuine smile.

These thoughts made her peep back at him with a tentative smile of her own. He was still regarding her, this time with a thoughtful expression on his lean features. 'Do you have the time to perhaps go for a walk down the beach with me?' she invited diffidently.

One corner of his mouth quirked as she watched. 'So I can protect you from the big black doggy?'

Laughing at him, she replied, 'Is that such a bad idea? No, I just thought a walk would be nice.' Greg shot another one of those piercing glances her way and instead of answering, turned and started to stroll towards the water.

Sara stood with the camera bag dangling from one slim hand and felt bereft as she watched him move away. He turned, saw her standing in an undecided attitude with dark hair blowing around her small face, and her large hazel eyes looking rather uncertain. A flash of white streaked across his face quickly, startling her with its attractive gleam, then was gone. 'You can leave your camera bag over in the ferns while we walk,' he told her. 'It'll be quite safe there.'

Her eyes lit up, and she ran back to the treeline quickly, depositing her bag and then running back. She didn't stop at his waiting figure but continued past until she reached the water's edge. Prompted by impulse, she bent and untied her shoes, stripping them and her socks off quickly, rolling her jeans up to her knees.

Two long legs joined her as she stooped and she sent a quick smile slanting up at Greg's watching eyes. 'I haven't been wading in the water yet, and I've been here for a week,' she remarked in explanation, and straightened. 'You could wade if you wanted to, and it wouldn't hurt those nice slacks if you roll them up enough so that they don't get wet.'

She didn't wait to see what he did but went into the cool water without hesitation. The hard wet sand gave way to soft, silky, shifting coolness, and she dug in her toes in appreciation. A wave crept up and licked delicately around her feet, receding almost immediately. Another came and lapped gently at her toes, and then another. She chuckled with pleasure and walked farther into the water until she was in up to her shins in a continuous push and pull from the ever-continuing waves that swirled about. She walked back to the shallow water, kicking over some stones, with her head bent to watch in the fading light for pretty flashes of colour. When she reached the sandy part of the wetness, past the row of small stones thrown up by waves, she stooped suddenly and dug in with both hands into the sand. Water crept up and touched her feet. She shot a sideways glance at the bare, dark brown shins that joined her in the water, then squatted back so that she could look up at Greg.

Her dark hair was falling like rain about her shoulders and over her forehead, and she used one arm to try and push it back, still clutching a handful of wet sand. He squatted with her and reached out one hand to push the hair away from her face gently. She smiled a thanks and dropped the sand, rinsing her hands quickly. 'Look,' she said softly, as a wave curled again about their feet, barely reaching them as it spent itself. She dug in again under the few inches of water and squeezed the wet sand through her fingers. It oozed delightfully, smooth and cool and very soft. 'Under the water everything's so magical and wonderful. It's just like silk, so soft and smooth. It's as fascinating as the bright glints of colour from the stones that flash under the water in the sunlight. They never look half as good dry and at home, did you ever notice? You take them away from the beach and you take all the magic away, all the fresh air and the crying birds and the cold clear water. When you pick up all this wonderful silk, this magical mess, it's just—mud.' She lifted up her two clenched hands again and let the brown sand plop into the shallow water.

Turning her head, she was strangely touched to see him reach out and dig his hand into the wet sand as if to see what she meant, his sombre expression lightening at the coolness of the water and the sensation she had so aptly described. He looked at his handful with something akin to fascination, then submerged the handful to clench his fist tight, squirting the sand and water.

Sara swished her hands around, the action like a small child playing in mud, then stood wiping her clean wet fingers on her jeans. One leg had fallen down and she rolled it up again before it could hit the water. Some distance away Beowulf was charging into the water and galloping back again, chasing waves and snapping jaws at the foamy water. She laughed and pointed him out to Greg.

'He's having almost as much fun as I am,' she told the silent man at her side with a chuckle. 'How silly we must look, playing in the water! I'd almost forgotten how much fun it could be. It seems like I've forgotten a lot lately, and only just came to my senses before plunging forever into a black darkness. Or better than that, I've escaped from a dark fortress and found sunlight for the first time in years. I've been such a fool! I wish I'd known how special my childhood was when I lived it! How wise children are, to enjoy the simple things.'

He hadn't said anything in reply, but merely watched her face intently, with a curious urgency. Sara gestured as she talked and looked around her, providing him with several different angles to observe her by. He watched the lively eyes and the slight tilt to her nose, and the smiling lips that were a darker shade of the rose that tinted her cheeks. In her eyes there shone a clear and peaceful expression, interspersed with amusement and sometimes mischief.

She felt good as Greg tucked her hand under his arm and directed her to walking parallel with the shore, water shooting up and swirling around them constantly. 'Our shoes?'

He looked back briefly. 'They'll be okay. They're past the waterline and won't get wet.'

She commented easily, 'Do you know, you're a total stranger to me? I don't even know your last name, and I didn't even know of your existence before this morning. Isn't that a funny thought? I've been talking to you with an appalling abandonment!'

The sun hung low over the water, she noticed. Its bottom curve nearly touched the horizon. The light was greying to her left and the treeline showed almost black. The dark head of the man beside her was tall and she looked up at the profile lit with the red of the fading light. A quick, neat turn of the head and he was staring down into her eyes and the shock of nearness, of his awareness cut through her like a knifing wind. 'My last name is Pierson,' he murmured quietly. 'But does it really matter?'

Those eyes, those warm, self-contained, lonely eyes. Sara shook her head slightly and his arm tightened on her hand. Is intuition ever correct? she wondered, shaken. If so, then I've known this man for ever, and everything else has been irrelevant. Their steps slowed.

'What I'm wondering,' he said thoughtfully, 'is why you look so curiously familiar to me.'

Realisation and sanity hit her like a blow and she jerked away on reflex. 'No reason.' It was only a whisper; for some reason she couldn't get out anything stronger. I don't know him, he doesn't know me. He really doesn't know me. Please, don't let him find out who I am. She started to hang back and took a few steps in the other direction. 'I'd better go.'

His hand whipped out. 'No, not yet,' he began. 'I'd like to . . .'

Far ahead, the black figure of the dancing dog suddenly stiffened, and a furious barking reached their ears. Greg also stiffened, in an attitude that seemed very reminiscent of his dog's, and he started forward to run swiftly down the beach. The dog shot to the treeline with a low menacing growl and Sara heard Greg shout directions at him, pointing up to the trees, and the dog changed direction, his great body leaping forcefully. Soon she heard sounds of yelling, and Greg too disappeared into the trees.

Feeling deeply alarmed, she ran forward too, straining to see what was going on under the shadow of the trees. She thought she saw a shorter dark figure dart forward and attach itself to a taller figure. The swiftly moving man she knew was Greg. Beowulf was attacking someone, a trespasser. She shouted sharply, 'Don't let him bite!'

A harsh order had Beowulf slinking back from the tall figure, and the strange man who had been attacked straightened, his breathing audible even from where she was. She faltered to a stop just behind Greg's shoulder, puzzled at his tenseness and very much frightened by the danger waves she was picking up from both him and the dog.

'What are you doing here?' The words came from Greg like the crack of a whip, and she jumped.

The other figure hesitated. "Just taking a walk,' came from the unknown other man. He was shorter than Greg.

'Where from?' Greg shot back.

'Up north,' the man told him, gesturing vaguely with one hand.

'That's private property too. What were you doing there?' Sara had never heard such an ugly tone of voice from Greg and she was growing more and more afraid without knowing why. The realisation that he truly was a stranger was brought home again forcibly when she heard him talk like this.

'Just exploring. I didn't mean any harm by it.' The tone from the other man was apologetic, placating.

Greg didn't appear to be mollified. 'I want you off the property in ten minutes,' he said evenly. Why was he in such a towering rage? He was standing very still and very stiff, Sara could feel it from where she stood. It impelled her to move, to place a tentative, soothing hand on the stiff shoulder just ahead. He shook it off impatiently, and she was so deeply hurt that she fell back. Wrong, she thought, wrong for me to feel this way. He's nothing but a stranger. Forget it. 'If you aren't off the property in ten minutes, I'll loose my dog after you. He knows how to search the grounds. Got that?'

'Look, mister, I didn't mean anything by——' The man was taking careful steps backwards.

'Get!' The word whipped the man into a faster pace, and he soon disappeared down the beach.

Greg stood watching him go, but Sara didn't wait to find out what happened. She turned and started running back the way they had come, moving as fast as she could. It shouldn't hurt this way, she thought dazedly, such disappointment in a stranger after all. I shouldn't care.

After a minute, Greg turned and saw the fleeing slight figure in the gathering darkness. 'Sara?' he called. 'Sara! Wait a moment, will you? Sara!'

She increased her pace until she was running as fast as she could, her breath coming heavily now from ploughing through the sand. She didn't seem to be going anywhere. It was like a nightmare that she had once had, of being chased and not being able to get anywhere though she tried and tried.

'Don't run so fast!' The words were shouted at her, and she heard pounding feet behind her. She knew he had to catch up with her soon. He was so much bigger and stronger for this kind of running and she was deplorably out of shape. Her chest heaved. 'You'll make yourself sick!'

What the devil does he mean? she had time to think before two hands hauled her to a stop. She stood with head bowed and chest heaving, the air coming from her in gasps. Greg stood with his hands on her shoulders, frowning at her, but she didn't see.

'Why did you run?' The tone sounded to her to be harsh and uncompromising, like the tone he had used with the strange man just now, and the shoulders that he held trembled in his grasp.

'M-my feet were cold,' she stammered, and gulped air. Her chest felt tight, and her head was beginning to ache behind the ears.

'You're lying to me,' Greg started, then stopped a second as he felt her involuntary cringe, so like her fear to the dog. He said slowly. 'Sara, are you afraid of me?'

The trembling seemed to increase at this, and she couldn't help it. His hands tightened. She thought a moment and decided that honesty was the best answer. 'Yes.'

Silence. Then, a more gentle tone, 'Why?'

'You—that man, I can't make any sense out of . . .' She made a huge effort and stopped for a minute with head bent, and took one sustaining breath. 'You were so hard on the man. I mean, I'm a trespasser, but you even invited me back, and he was just taking a walk on the beach, and you were going to loose the dog on him, and——'

'You,' Greg told her, 'couldn't hurt a flea, and we both know that. Furthermore,' and his grip tightened on her shoulders and drew her near him. She resisted, but he drew her near anyway, 'I happen to know my neighbours in the north, and he wasn't any of them. He was a stranger and he was trespassing deep into private property. He was not on the beach but on a path that leads to my house, and he had no business up there. If he'd been on the beach it might have been different. You, I know, are harmless, while he's virtually unknown . . .

'How?' she burst out, staring up into the darkness where his face was supposed to be. One part of her brain thought, God, I'm shaken.

'I checked on you this afternoon,' he said simply. 'You really are a neighbour who's rented the cabin for six months. Your landlord even told me that you were right when you said there were two fireplaces and no firewood.'

'I burned my cigarettes this afternoon,' she murmured, apparently irrelevantly. The hands loosened on her shoulders and one arm replaced them, drawing her into his side and held to his body warmth in a quick hug.

'Good girl!'

Then she exploded. 'My God, what gives you the right to think *you* need to check up on me, when you're acting a damned sight fishier than I am, for heaven's sake, and all I did was trespass a few hundred yards, and you're probably going to be responsible for a murder if you loose your horrid dog on that fellow, because you *know* that he won't have enough time to get off the property before then, it's much too big . . .'

She was stopped, very effectively, by warm lips that took her mouth in a long, hard kiss that seemed to shock all of the breath out of her. When that dark head lifted from her, all she could do was stare.

'I wanted to do that when you picked up the sand with both fists,' he said in a voice that sounded as if he was discussing the weather.

Sara murmured, 'It was nice.' Greg's arm came around her again and tightened. He started to walk her slowly, keeping her close to his side. She didn't object. She should have, probably, but she didn't. Instead, she snuggled closer.

'Did you hurt yourself?' he asked her.

'What?'

'When you ran so hard. You said to me that you were recuperating from an illness and I was worried that you would do yourself harm by running so recklessly.'

'Oh,' she said, and then, 'oh, no, I hadn't broken any bones or anything like that. It was—more a virus, you know. I've quite recovered from it.'

'When do you go back to your work?' a quiet voice had asked her, and the question was so close to her own thoughts that she jumped violently.

'I'm not sure,' she said hesitantly, wondering what to say next. 'It kind of depends on how well I recuperate, you see, and if I get bored soon. It may be a few months.'

'Were you smart to go wading into the cold water like you did? Could it bring back the virus you had?'

Sara answered this truthfully. 'I never even thought of it.' The arm around her tightened again.

'You need a nursemaid to take care of you if you're going to be this irresponsible,' he told her, and she put a hand to her mouth to keep from laughing aloud.

They found their shoes quickly in the moonlight, and both had to sit on the sand to put them on. She made a comment about his nice slacks, which he promptly told her not to worry about, and they both sat looking over the dark water that occasionally sparkled from the pale light that gently suffused the October night. The air was getting nippy; even though the days were just like summer with an unseasonal heat, the nights were getting distinctly chilly.

The water lapping so gently seemed to have her falling into a trance. She lay back on the soft sand and stared up at the sky. The man beside her was silent, almost totally black, and she wondered that she would feel alternately so comfortable with him and at the same time so uneasy. She wondered why he was so distinctly unfriendly to strangers, or why he would want to check up on a neighbour with very little provocation. She decided that he must be either very rich, or illegal, and possibly both. She decided that she didn't want to know.

'I want a cigarette so badly, I can just taste what it would be like,' she told him conversationally. 'That marvellous smell, the relaxation . . .'

'. . . the smoke damage to your lungs, the heart problems . . .' added Greg with what sounded like a smile in his voice.

'. . . the tantalising curl of the smoke from the glowing end, such pleasure . . .' she murmured, and laughed. 'It's a good thing I burned my carton of cigarettes! Now there aren't any in the house—oh, wonderful! I forgot to check the glove compartment of my car, and I always keep a pack there. I'll have to go and get them.' She didn't move, in spite of the craving her body felt.

'You don't need them. Throw them out!' he told her, propping himself up on one elbow to look down on her face. The moonlight on her skin made it look like polished marble, and her eyes glittered like liquid jewels. 'Why should you need artificial stimulation or a depressant? You seem like you can get your happiness

well enough on your own. Make in on your own steam,
don't rely on drugs.'

The marble smoothness of her face cracked, and as
he watched, the liquid quality of her gleaming eyes
shimmered and two sparkling tears slid down her
cheeks. The eyes closed, hiding those expressive orbs.
Then, with a sudden movement, she rolled over in the
sand and hid her face in her arms to weep.

Greg moved close, shocked. 'What did I say?' he
asked her lowly, putting out a hand to lay on those
shaking shoulders. They felt so thin! 'What did I do?'

After a little, Sara whispered, 'It isn't you, it's me.'

'What did you do?' The question was asked gently.
The hand on her shoulder rubbed up and down,
soothing and comforting.

At that, she rolled back over and stared up at the sky,
feeling after that first bit of terrible sadness a surprising
measure of calm. 'I've been a fool, that's all,' she said,
smiling a little. 'It's hard to admit when you've been a
fool, and often you don't feel proud of yourself. When I
was sick, before I knew it, I was feeling really tired and
draggy, really down. I could barely get through work.
Someone offered me a pill. I guess it was speed. I
wanted to take it so badly, and I've always been very
careful as to what I put in my body and there I was,
wanting to take that pill. I told myself that it was only
one, that it wouldn't really make any difference. Of
course that's not true. It's not the pill that matters, but
the reasons and philosophies behind it.'

He was very still, and when she paused, his low voice
prompted gently, 'And did you take it?'

'No,' she sighed, stirring. 'But that was when I realised
that something was terribly wrong in my life, and that's
why I'm changing it right now. There for a while I was
afraid I'd lost myself somewhere along the way.'

'And do you think you've found yourself again?' She
turned her head to look at Greg.

'I think so. I'm not sure. I guess so, if you count gaining back some measure of calm and peace. I'm still looking for my self-respect—I really misplaced that one.' Silence settled on them for a time. Sara felt reluctant to move. The peace that she had mentioned came to her now and settled on her like a comforter, warming her with serenity.

She felt so good, sitting on the beach with this man. She felt more comfortable with him than she had ever felt with Barry or any of her musicians or acquaintances. There he was, like some black monolith in the night, and she didn't know a thing about him, but his understanding questions and gentle touch had meant more to her than any overtures that she had been the recipient of for the past six years. It was because he gave them straight from himself to herself. There was no barrier, no underlying motive stemming from who she was, or how influential she could be with the company she worked with—or was there?

She kept very still on the sand as her brain started to click over certain things with an uncomfortable suspicion. Suddenly she remembered the odd way that Greg had looked at her when she had first arrived on the scene that morning and had built the sand castle. His gaze had been very keen and piercing. Sara knew that her face was extremely well known, and the bone structure so prominent as to make her face probably distinctive enough to make one wonder. And he had admittedly 'checked up' on her residence. Just how far had that check-up gone? If he had enquired into her past work position or residence, then he would have come up with a complete blank. Sara Carmichael didn't really exist in a practical sense, for Sara Bertelli had lived for six years in California. If Greg had made the least push to find out what she did for a living, he would have her, for she had no work history, and her landlord knew nothing. If he got suspicious enough to check that far, then the fact that Sara Carmichael didn't really exist as far as records go would be enough to make him turn ugly with suspicion—for he was so wary of strangers that he must be hiding something, what she didn't know, but he was definitely hiding something— or it would be enough to push his memory to the truth. Without her heavy make-up she could fob off casual glances her way, but she couldn't hope to do it with a discerning eye.

One thing that had struck her about Greg was that he had a definite discerning eye. He noticed everything, like a hawk.

It was a suspicion on her part, but it was such a strong suspicion, and she had taken so much pleasure in thinking that they had dealt well together, just themselves with no pretence or pressure, that she closed her eyes against it. It was too late, however, and had been too late the moment the thought had entered her mind. The unpleasant part about the whole thing was that she felt so naked, so completely vulnerable now, that she would not feel comfortable around him whether he really knew or not. Just that she would suspect it was enough to destroy whatever natural attitude she had been able to adopt around him, because she knew that she could never ask him for the truth.

She sat up, staring out in the early evening, blinking like a sleepwalker newly awakened. The night lost all of its magic and its peace and a perfect day was ruined.

She mumbled, 'I'm going home,' and stood, looking around her and trying to remember just where she had put her camera bag. It was so dark that she couldn't see landmarks very well.

'This is abrupt,' he said, and stood also. Looking down at her and trying to catch a glimpse of her face, he asked her. 'Something wrong?'

She was twisting around, trying to keep her face

hidden from him, and she asked him, 'Can you remember where I left my camera bag?' She walked away from him in a way that suggested hurry. Greg stood very still and watched her.

'No, I don't.'

'It's so dark that I can't see where I left it,' she remarked, using the excuse to move even further away from him. The problem was that he followed. She backed up again.

'I could bring it to you in the morning,' Greg offered quietly.

'No! That's all right,' she tried to mollify her terse answer. 'I think I can find it, and I don't want you to go to any trouble on my account.' Why did he make her feel so threatened?

'It's no trouble,' he was still quiet, and very still.

Sara turned and abandoned the conversation, just leaving Greg where he stood. She went to the bushes and started to feel around with her hands, remembering that it was somewhere near the edge and just out of casual sight. She heard footsteps behind her and refused to look up.

'What happened?' the quiet voice came to her. She stopped looking a moment and then continued, her mouth dry and hands shaking. Ever since she had started to entertain doubts about him, it had thrown all their conversations into a different light. What if he was a reporter? What if he was sent by Barry to keep an eye on her? It was something that Barry would do.

'What do you mean?' she asked, stalling for time. Her groping hands found the bulky bag, and she swung it up to her shoulder with relief. She had to get out of there; she had to get away from this man.

'What happened just now? Something did, what I don't know, but I can tell you just when it did. You've thought of something, and you're shying away like a startled rabbit.' That quiet voice could be so terrible, she found, listening to it with ears pricked with fear. 'What did you think of, Sara? Has something started to bother you? Have you forgotten to tell me something about yourself, like, are you a reporter out for a story?'

'What?' she gasped, astounded. It was so close to what she had been thinking that she sagged from the shock. Then she remembered. She had been acting oddly, and if Greg was involved with something illegal like she suspected then he wouldn't want reporters around any more than she would. Of course he'd be suspicious. 'No, I'm not a reporter. I just want to go home.'

'Then I'll walk you.' In spite of all her protests, he did accompany her on her walk with a pleasantness she didn't find at all relaxing. Never had that five-minute walk from the beach to her back door seemed so long or so uncomfortable. He asked her all sorts of searching questions, and she fumbled through most of them like a first-grade girl caught lying. Thrown off balance and feeling immeasurably shaken up by his curiously menacing attitude, she couldn't think how to answer some of his more pressing questions. She finally flared up at him in anger, telling him to leave her alone, and whirled away to sweep into her house and lock the door behind her with a trembling hand.

# CHAPTER THREE

INSIDE the door, Sara leaned up weakly against the wall, listening for sounds from outside. She couldn't hear any, and moving to the curtained window, she twitched it aside to peer from the darkened kitchen into the equally dark night. There was nobody there, and that was why she felt so shocked when she glanced casually out the front window before retiring to bed and saw a tall dark shadow just off the road and under the trees. He appeared to be staring at the cabin, and she backed away from the door in a panic, in spite of knowing that he couldn't see her.

Just knowing that Greg was watching the house made her rush around, bolting the front and back doors in addition to locking them, and she made sure that every window was closed and latched. Then, sitting on her couch in an empty, cold living room, she stared into space, shivering.

She finally went to bed late that night and as a result slept heavily and deeply into the morning. It was eleven o'clock before she even opened her eyes. A depression settled over her when she realised the time. What did she have to get up for? Where did she have to go? Whom did she get to look forward to meeting? These questions and others plagued her throughout the small remainder of the morning. She didn't bother to get dressed; she wasn't going to get out of the house, and no one would be seeing her.

After feeling so good about herself for a long stretch of time, this depression hit her hard. She listlessly made herself a cup of tea and took it into the living room. Setting the cup down on the coffee table, she took the time to belt her dressing gown more firmly around her small waist before sitting down. Just as she was sinking into a curled-up position on the couch, a firm knock sounded at the front door, making her nearly jump out of her skin. She stared at the rectangular frame of wood, as if expecting someone to bash down the door and force an entry into the house. Who in the world could be wanting to see her? Perhaps it was someone who had taken a wrong turn off the nearby highway, and wanted to know directions. Sara considered this possibility for a moment with her head cocked to one side, as the knocking turned to imperative pounding, and she decided that it couldn't be that. The road was little more than a hard-packed dirt path, and was obscure. It was impossible to mistake the way, and impossible not to find the way back to the highway. All one had to do was turn around.

She slipped quietly up to the door and peered through the peephole with curiosity—then recoiled as if stung. Greg's tall commanding frame fully filled the small magnifying glass, his dark face looking sombre, even stern. She didn't like that look. It frightened her. She backed away from the door and climbed on to the couch slowly, watching her front curtained windows as if she expected him to crash into the room. He didn't, but the pounding continued for some minutes, along with his deep voice calling her.

'Sara? Sara!' he shouted through the door. 'I know you're in there, because your car is in the garage. Let me in, please! I want to talk to you. Sara? Are you all right?'

She picked up her cup of tea and sipped it carefully, listening to his calling. Finally, seemingly to take ages in her mind, the calling stopped and footsteps sounded on the small wooden porch. She sighed and began to relax, only just then realising how tensely she had been holding herself. That was why when she heard hard knocking at her back door, and the rattle of her door knob, she jumped like a startled colt. Unable to help herself, she crept into the kitchen to listen to Greg calling to her, a thread of impatience running through his deep voice. Eventually he stopped, and she went about the small routine of fixing herself another cup of tea. After staring at the wall opposite the couch for quite some time and consuming several cups of tea, she finally managed to rouse herself enough to take a shower. Leaving her hair wet and hanging limply down her back, with the dressing gown belted once more about her waist, she padded into the living room, seating herself at the old upright piano and stared at the keys with sadness.

She wanted to play but couldn't seem to find it within herself. She wanted to be creative and work out a new, strange melody to adequately describe just what she was feeling inside, but she couldn't seem to pick up her heavy hands and play. She wanted to sing, to pour out her guts and to fill the room with her voice, to release all that was inside and aching to get out, but the music just wasn't there. For the first time in her life, Sara couldn't play.

She sat looking down at her hands, and tears slid down her face. What had she done to herself? Had she really damaged her own music beyond repair? She couldn't accept that. Her music would always be with her. It was as much a part of herself as her breathing and thinking. She would only lose her music when she laid down her head and died. Somewhere, deep down inside, it was still living.

One hand tentatively reached out to caress the keyboard with a reverent, loving finger. She loved it so. She would never, ever sacrifice her own desires to play what others wanted to hear. She would make music only for her own fulfilment, and offer that to the public. She would play now, only for herself. Both hands came to rest on the keys, and she flexed her fingers, once, twice. Then a resounding crash filled the room as she played a half-forgotten melody that she had written years ago. It had never gone beyond the stage of pure sound and personal satisfaction, and she was suddenly very glad for it. It was her own song, nobody else's. She had not sold it for money; it belonged only to her.

She faltered through the execution of the melody, stopping several times to go back over certain parts of it again, refreshing her memory and reviving the song. She had written it in a furious burst of anger when she was barely twenty. Her mother had just died, and all Sara's pain, grief, and anguish had spilled into the song. Playing it now was like some kind of purge to her soul. It cleaned her out and filled her up again with something new.

Afterwards, feeling hungry for the first time that day, she went to the kitchen and ate a hearty meal. The afternoon was fast disappearing, and she turned on a table lamp in the living room and prepared to settle down with a good book.

She had just barely begun to read when a knocking sounded again at her door. Should she answer? She didn't particularly want to see anyone. Greg's voice sounded through the door, and she detected a note of anxiety. 'Sara? I hoped to see you on the beach today. Are you not feeling well? Can I help you in any way? Do you need a doctor?'

As she listened, strangely touched by his concern, slow tears filled her eyes, but she wouldn't let them overflow. She had to blink rapidly to make her vision clear. Why should he care? Was this just a ruse to get her to open the door?

Footsteps sounded on the front porch like they had this morning when Greg had gone away, but she began to hear funny noises, things being pounded against the outside wall just back from the porch. It sounded as if he was hitting something in between the back door and the stone fireplace, to the left of the house. Eventually overcome by curiosity, Sara slipped into the kitchen and tried to peep out of the curtained window, but she couldn't see anything. The footsteps were making regular, short trips back and forth, and it sounded as if there was something metal outside.

She slowly slid back the bolt and turned the lock in the doorknob, still listening intently. Grasping the handle and turning it, she pulled the door open quietly to peer outside, her half wet hair hanging around her in a tumbled mess and her large eyes uncertain, wary. She saw Greg approaching her way from a pick-up truck, his powerful arms filled with neatly cut firewood. He already had a nice amount carefully stacked against the house. He in turn saw her head and one shoulder peek around the half-opened door, and he took in the large, startled look in her eyes, the pale skin, and the slight circles underneath those huge questioning orbs. She looked like a small, puzzled child.

Setting down the firewood in a careful movement, he made no immediate attempt to come nearer to her, for she looked as if she might bolt and slam the door shut at any sudden action. 'Hello,' he said calmly, as if talking to an unsettled horse. 'I remembered that you said you needed firewood, and I had a few trees I've been planning to get rid of for some time. Is it all right stacked here, or do you want it someplace else?

'What?' she asked, feeling stupid. She felt stunned at this uncalled-for gesture of goodwill, and edged a little further from behind the door. Greg saw that she was in a quilted dressing gown that fell nearly to the floor. Bare toes peeped from underneath.

He took an involuntary step forward. 'You've been sick? Are you all right?' His voice sounded sharp from anxiety.

Sara took a hasty step backwards, shaking her head

until her hair tumbled about. 'No, I'm fine,' she murmured uneasily. 'Really I am.'

Her eyes watched him with that same puzzlement, as if she expected him to sprout four legs and a tail right there on the spot. He looked very good to her. His faded and tight jeans were streaked here and there, and his plaid flannel shirt strained across broad shoulders and was rolled up at the sleeves to past his elbows. She could just imagine him wielding a heavy axe with ease. He would be good at it, she thought. His hard face held a strange expression, almost forbidding, with that dark searching gaze, the hard mouth held firm, the jaw strong.

'Don't look at me like that!' he said abruptly, taking another experimental step forward. She didn't back away this time.

'Like what?' Why was she acting so stupidly this afternoon? She couldn't tear her eyes away from his face; it seemed too important.

'Like you expect me to hit you in the face!' he uttered forcefully. 'I was worried when you didn't answer the door.'

'Why?' she asked him baldly. She wanted to take his words at face value so badly, and she didn't know if she dared.

'Because you're so isolated here and so vulnerable, I——' He took a deep breath. 'You'd been ill, and I was worried that you'd had a relapse.'

'I didn't want to see you!' she burst out, and suddenly felt as if she had gone mute. She couldn't for the life of her think of something else to say.

'I know.' His own reply was low. He had winced when she had blurted out her confession, and she felt absolutely terrible. The day was grey and dreary and a nippy wind blew about her feet, making her shiver. Greg took a quick comprehensive glance at her bare feet, her damp hair and her shivers, and told her quickly, 'Go on inside and I'll finish stacking the wood against the house. I'll knock and let you know when I'm done, and bring in some wood to stack by the fireplace, if you like.'

'Why,' she asked impulsively, shaking as a wind hit her exposed head. 'are you being so nice to me? Why are you doing this?'

He merely shook his head with a faint smile, and told her, 'Shut that door before you catch your death. Hurry now, we'll talk later.'

Feeling more and more chilled by the second, Sara hastened to do as he said. Funny, she thought, shutting the door behind her and rushing through the kitchen with the sudden desire to get dressed and dry her hair, how the day had suddenly turned into a nice one after all. She pulled on a black pair of jeans and drew on a pretty blouse with a high collar and an edge of lace around the neck and wrists, and pulled on a pale peach sweater over it. Brushing her hair briskly, she held a hand dryer to her head for a few minutes, then threw it down in disgust. She didn't have the patience for that. She picked up her blusher and stroked a little colour over her cheekbones, then touched her eyelids with a dark blue shadow that made her eyes appear as a vivid blue. After looking at herself closely in the mirror, she rubbed off a little of the eye-shadow. She wanted to look good, but she didn't want him to think that she had put on make-up for his sake, even though she had. She touched her lashes with a brown mascara so that they looked longer but still natural, then hurried outside.

Greg was nearing the end of the huge stack of wood in the back of the truck, and he turned when he heard the back door open to smile down at her. He was standing in the bed of the truck, and his feet were spread wide apart for balance. His brown hair fell across his forehead and his big hands were dusty. Sara blinked up at him; when he smiled it changed his entire aspect and made that stern, almost menacing image fade completely away. It eased the hardness from an already harsh visage.

'How old are you?' she asked irrelevantly.

His firm lips quirked into a wider smile. 'Thirty-three.'

'You seem older,' she told him, cocking her head to one side in an attitude of perusal, appraisal. 'It's not exactly your features, but that look you wear when you aren't aware of being watched. You—look more mature, as if you've lived a lot.' Suddenly aware of how personal she had become, she flushed quickly and said, 'But it's none of my business, I shouldn't have made such a comment.'

She was looking down, afraid of a rebuff and worrying that perhaps she had earned it, when a large hand came to her small chin and tilted her face up. There was a gentle look in his eyes as he told her, 'You don't look as if you could be twenty-one, let alone twenty-eight. Are you pulling my leg?'

Again she flushed, but this time it was with pleasure, and she gave a little laugh. 'No, unfortunately not, I am twenty-eight. I used to wear a lot of make-up so that I looked older, because I've always looked more immature than everyone else my age, and it made me selfconscious. Now I don't care any more.'

Greg let his eyes travel over Sara's face, and a look of puzzlement crossed his. 'I can't figure out why you look so familiar to me,' he said almost to himself. 'It keeps coming to mind. Who are you, Sara Carmichael?'

She dropped her eyes, at once happy and yet unhappy. If he was being truthful right now, then her suspicions of last night night were invalid. She so hoped that he was being truthful. 'Who are you, Greg Pierson?' she countered lightly.

The hand at her chin moved in a caressing gesture. It

felt so good that she swallowed, afraid to move and
break the contact. 'Why did you run away last night?'
he asked gently.

A frown creased the smooth wide expanse of her
forehead, and her eyes fluttered up to touch on his
quizzical gaze, then fell away. Then, with an honesty that
sounded so totally real and unfaked, she shrugged and
said, 'You scared me. I don't know, I might have scared
myself a little. You seemed so—big and menacing all of
a sudden, and I just ran away.' Then, with a hint of
desperation colouring her voice, she whispered, 'I only
met you yesterday!'

'I know,' he murmured, his hand still at her throat
and almost encircling it, and yet she felt no uneasiness
at her own vulnerability, for his touch was so gentle and
light, the thumb moving in a small circle on the pulse at
the base of her throat. 'I'm sorry for being so nasty to
you last night. I've been off balance for a while and
took out my uncharitable feelings for mankind on you.'
The hand was lifted away abruptly and her eyes flew to
his at the sudden movement. 'My hands are so dirty,
I've just made your neck all smudged.'

She suspected that, in that small apology and
confession, Greg had told her a great deal about
himself, and she realised that it couldn't have been easy
for him. Not easy at all, if he had to climb over that
great wall he had around himself that excluded the
world. He must have been badly hurt at one time, so
badly hurt that he'd had to defend himself with
hostility, lashing out to avoid ever being that badly hurt
again. It was all conjecture on her part, based on a two-
sentence speech and a certain look of pain in his eyes,
but it made her voice soften to him as she replied, 'I'll
wash clean, don't worry. Can I help you?'

'Not in that pretty sweater,' he told her. 'If you could
go and open that door to the living room, I'll carry in
some wood for you. Do you have a wood box?'

'Yes.' She moved away as she spoke. 'And it's probably totally empty except for a few spiders. I'll go and get the door.'

She ran lightly inside and passed through the cabin to unlock the front door. Then she cast a quick glance around her as she did so; the living room looked charming, though small, and there wasn't anything she needed to tidy up. She called out to Greg, then went to see if there was anything in the box that was positioned by the fireplace. She had lifted up the lid and was peering doubtfully into its depths when heavy footsteps sounded on the porch and Greg came inside with a load of wood.

'Does it look all right?' he asked her, a little thread of amusement running through his pleasant voice as he surveyed her stooping figure and uncertain expression.

She looked up, grinning. How could I have ever imagined that voice hard and cold? she asked herself. 'There doesn't seem to be a family nesting inside, so I guess it's safe enough.'

Stepping nimbly back, she watched him dump his load into the box. As he straightened and headed out of the door for more, she called after him, 'How would you like something hot to drink after you finish?'

A brief glance over broad shoulders had dark eyes sparkling at her. 'That would be very nice, thank you. It'll take me about two more trips to get this box full, so I'll be about five minutes.'

'Fine, then I'll go ahead and put on a pot of coffee. Or would you like tea instead?' Sara flung her hair off her face as she spoke and noticed his eyes touching on her shoulders as it settled back.

'Coffee's fine.' Greg was quickly outside again, and she left to go and plug in her coffeemaker. She was rummaging around in her refrigerator when Greg spoke from the doorway. 'Where can I wash?'

She put down the packages that she had hauled out

and went to the doorway to stand near him, peering around the corner and pointing out the door. As she stuck her head around and turned her face away from him, she felt a hand in her hair at the back of her head, and looked up enquiringly. 'Is something wrong?' He was very close, she realised belatedly, and seemed stronger than ever in such proximity, and larger. His face was bent towards her, and she ran her hand over the jutting bones under the tanned skin. His lower cheeks and chin were getting the finest spinkle of beard, and she wanted to reach up and scratch her fingers on it.

'Just looking to see if your hair is dry yet,' he replied, running his hand through the strands slowly. He frowned. Her hair was still damp, being so long and thick, and the strands felt cold to the touch. 'You really should blow your hair dry. What if you get sick again? There aren't any neighbours within calling distance, and you'd be quite alone if anything happened.'

She answered easily, 'I'll just make a list of emergency numbers, then. Don't worry so much! I've been alone for years and nothing has happened to me yet.' Her eyes moved to the phone book that sat in a little cubbyhole just under the cabin's only phone. Walking over thoughtfully, she pulled out the book and started to leaf slowly through the pages.

Greg had watched her without going to wash, and he asked her curiously, 'Who are you going to call?'

'Hmm? No one, just yet,' she murmured, still thinking over whatever had crossed her mind, and not really paying attention to him as he came to stand just by her shoulder. 'I just thought I'd make a list of emergency numbers so I would have at my fingertips someone to call if I'm in trouble.' She didn't look up, pointing with a forefinger to the inside flap of the book. 'It looks as though there's already a list made out in front.'

Greg was still frowning thoughtfully as he perused

the numbers. 'It would take time for these people to get here—look, that hospital number is a different area, at least half an hour's drive away. Can I give you my number to call if you need anything? I can be over here in less than ten minutes if anything is wrong.'

Sara felt vastly touched by this. 'Greg, that's very good of you. If you really don't mind the bother——'

His lips pulled into a crooked smile. 'No bother, sweetheart. Just jot this down, and I'll go and clean up . . .' She scribbled the number that he gave her, and as he disappeared down the hall, she went back to making sandwiches with a warm feeling inside. He was soon entering the kitchen with his dark hair neat and his hands scrubbed clean, and slowed at the doorway when he found her with a secret little quirk of the mouth that he discovered was deliciously tantalising. 'Good joke, I take it?' the deep voice sounded right behind her, and she whirled. Chuckling at the expression on her face, Greg looked past her at the array of sandwiches and the steaming coffee and murmured appreciatively, 'A feast for a starving man!'

'Help yourself,' she invited, pulling out a chair for him and laughing when he sat down. He looked up enquiringly, one dark brow up.

'Am I the cause of that laughter?'

'In a way. You make this kitchen seem so small, and that chair positively groaned when you sat in it,' she told him with twinkling eyes. 'I guess I hadn't realised how big you really are.'

In response to her good humour, he suddenly smiled. Sara couldn't seem to take her eyes off his strong features. While he ate, she sipped coffee, and they talked about light things, but she got the strangest feeling as they relaxed together. It was as if they were really saying something else, something deeper to each other. Sara looked up from her coffee quickly once and found his eyes on her in the most intent and gentle way.

Good heavens, she thought, as she suddenly felt as if she were drowning in that gaze, what's happening to me? I had no idea he could be so—her thoughts stopped, and she searched for something to say.

'I—I saw you outside last night,' she commented at random, and the gentle look in his eyes was slowly replaced with a look of puzzlement.

'I'm not sure I know what you mean.'

It was her turn to feel a slight puzzlement and she explained, 'Out in the front yard, after I went inside, were you—walking around about half an hour later?'

He frowned. 'I went right home. Are you sure you saw something?'

She sat very still and thought over the last night, and gradually a cold chill crept over her. There had been a dark figure out front, she felt sure, and the realisation that it hadn't been Greg after all put an entirely different light on the situation. She had completely forgotten that she had been afraid enough when she had thought that it was him. Standing abruptly, she went into the living room to stare out of the front picture window. The direction of her gaze showed her that there was nothing where a tall figure had been before, no brush or bush or tree that could be misconstrued as something else. There had been someone there last night—she was sure of it. A hand touched her shoulder and she jumped violently. Without looking around, she became aware that Greg was very close. She could feel his body heat at her back, and on impulse she leaned back against his chest. He immediately put his arms around her, and it felt so good and warm and right that she sighed, closing her eyes. A slight pressure at the side of her head told her that he was leaning his cheek against her hair. She had never felt so small and vulnerable and yet so safe, before in her life. Greg was very careful in how he held her; she could feel the restrained power in his arms. They stood this way for a long time.

'There was someone out there last night, Greg—I swear it.'

His arms tightened and his head went up as he too looked out the window. 'Where?'

She pointed out the spot to him, for some reason unable to feel the alarm that had been so apparent just minutes before. Greg's presence was too immediate and overwhelming to her. He looked out the window for a minute, and when she tilted her head back on his shoulder to see his expression, he quickly smiled reassuringly and dropped a kiss on her nose. 'I need to get going, I'm afraid—got a lot of things to do, and Beowulf is penned up. He needs a meal and a run. Would you like me to stop by later this evening, and have a look around outside, just in case?'

Sara looked up gratefully at him. 'I'd appreciate it if you did. I'd feel much better about things, really.'

'I'll knock at your front door, then, and let you know that it's me prowling about outside, so that you don't faint from shock, all right?'

She nodded, and a strange look came over his face, a brooding look that was almost hostile. It was as if a shutter had come down over his features, masking his thoughts from the outer world. She had begun to know him better, though, and to understand him in an instinctive way. She knew enough to look beyond that careful mask, and she saw his dark eyes watching her with great attention. Intuitively guessing his feelings, she ignored that brooding look and went up to him to put a light hand on his arm with a smile.

'I really am fine, you know,' she murmured. 'Don't worry about me.'

His body relaxed, though his face didn't change. He said abruptly. It's just that when you didn't answer the door today, I started to wonder ... call me if you need anything.'

'I will.'

She walked him to the front door, thanking him again for the firewood. He turned back to answer her, his eyes smiling again in that subtle way, then his eyes lit upon the upright piano. 'Oh, was that left here with the furniture?' he asked idly, flicking a careless hand to it. Sara turned to see what he had meant and stiffened. It was an involuntary reaction, and she couldn't help herself even though she knew that he had sensed her strange behaviour and was looking at her oddly.

'No,' she replied shortly, moving away. 'It's mine. I had it brought in when I moved.' To tell the truth, she owned three pianos, all in vastly better shape and quality than this one, but she had bought it for temporary use, not wanting to ship hers halfway across America.

Greg was watching her with an interested look. 'So you play. Are you good?' He looked thoughtful and she felt suddenly desperate to wipe that look off his face. She didn't want him to find out who she was just yet. It would cause a rift, either in his thinking or in hers. He would back away from her like a cat landing on hot bricks, she guessed, because of her exposure to the public, or she would run away from him in a panic, afraid that she would never know his motives for continuing their relationship were he to discover her real identity.

'So-so,' she muttered, then she said quickly. 'Maybe some day I'll practice up and play you something. I'm rusty at the moment.' It's true, she argued silently with herself. I am out of practice. This silent argument didn't assuage her sense of guilt, for she knew she had let him think that she was a bashful amateur. Her own concept of being out of practice was totally out of the league that she had implied to him she was in. She could sit at that piano and play with a passionate grace at any given time. The tiny mistakes that she would be apt to make would not be noticed by a normal listener.

Greg was smiling down at her easily. Was it just her imagination or did something flit across his face? 'Maybe some time you could. I'd like that—I'm quite a music lover.'

'Oh no!' she groaned involuntarily, and he looked at her with both brows up. She added hastily, 'I bet that means you're an intelligent and informed critic and you only listen to the masters in the field. Now you'll never get me to play!' A good excuse, she congratulated herself. Without conceit, she knew that she had a distinctive style, and she didn't want to try to put him off with a clumsy attempt to play either badly or in another style.

'But I would take into account your experience and not judge you unfairly,' he promised, with a curious smile.

'I'll bet,' she retorted, and laughed. 'Enough! I have work to do and you have a starving dog, so I don't want to hear any more. See you.'

She leaned weakly against the door after he left. 'Fool!' she berated herself angrily, and the sound of her own voice was so loud in the suddenly silent house that she jumped. Why, oh, why hadn't she lied when he asked her who owned the piano? Was it that she secretly hoped he would guess the truth about her and demonstrate how little it mattered to him? Did she hope that if she gave him some subtle clue as to who she was, he would sooner or later recognise her? Was it a cowardly way of letting him know the truth and yet getting out of having to tell him personally? Whatever the reason, it was too late to change what had happened. She would have to wait and see. Time would tell whether he recognised her or not.

She was so agitated that she started to pace the living room back and forth. It took her exactly seven good sized paces to cover the open area, then she turned to pace the seven steps back. She noted this with one detached corner of her mind in the crazy, irrelevant way she had whenever she was really upset. It was solemnly filed away for future reference. The other part of her mind told herself emphatically just how stupid she was to be paying so much attention to such a trivial detail while she had other more important things to think about. But she couldn't help counting the steps once she had made the observation. It was like a tape recording playing over and over again: Seven *up*, seven *back*, five to the *front* door and then seven *up*, seven *back* ... She forced herself to stop and sit down in an effort to think calmly. Greg Pierson, a man with shadowed eyes, shadowed past, shadowed motives. What did she really know about him? Materially, nothing.

A tiny voice whispered, his eyes are warm. She shook her head so violently that her hair whipped around and caught on her eyelashes. Raising a hand to push it away impatiently, she stared out of the picture window at the grey day. Would it rain?

He's strong, that little voice whispered to her. Sara gave a short mirthless laugh. If she didn't stop this soon they would be taking her away in a straitjacket! Pretty soon she would be talking to people who weren't really there, and she promptly said aloud, 'So what?' Her serious thoughts gave way to a little bit of giggling, and she shook herself mentally, going into the kitchen to wash up the few dishes that had been dirtied. She took an excessive amount of time with the two coffee mugs. She had bought them in Mexico a few years ago, and they were hand-crafted, very pretty.

He is gentle with you, and concerned, that small voice spoke again. The still quiet knowledge could not be denied, and she sank slowly into a chair, the dish cloth in her hands, twisted and unnoticed.

She let herself think of him freely then, without trying
to escape from the direction her thoughts were leading
her to. It was, she mused, too late for her. It had been
too late when she had looked into Greg's eyes and had
seen him smile that first heart-stopping time. What kind
of fool was she? She had become infatuated with a total
stranger without a second's resistance.

She was twenty-eight. She was lonely. So what?
Many people are. She had been lonely for most of her
life. What was so different now?

She was eager for some kind of meaningful
relationship for a change, instead of the sterile empty
acquaintances she'd known for so many years. She
wanted the pain and the pleasure of giving and taking,
learning and loving. That she would fall for the first
decent specimen that stumbled her way without
knowing who she really was! What would he think of
her if he knew? That had her smiling grimly. She could
imagine what he might say. A more amusing thought
struck her then: what would Barry think?

He would, she thought crudely, have a hissy fit, and
the thought made her laugh aloud. 'God, Sara!' he
would expostulate. 'Don't you know enough not to get
emotionally involved with a vacation fling? Baby,
you've gone right around the bend!'

Someone knocked on her front door and she
moved swiftly to answer. Greg, she thought, but when
she swung the door open and smiled widely at the
man standing on her porch, her grin of delight
quickly turned to a blank stare of astonishment and
dismay.

'Hello, love,' said Barry, shuffling his feet nervously
and smiling tentatively at her expression. 'Can I—er—
come in?'

'Oh, good grief!' she groaned, letting the door knob
slip from her nerveless fingers. The door, left to swing
by itself, gently swished and knocked against the wall,

and she automatically caught it on the return swing.
'Just what in sweet tropical hell are you doing here?'

'I knew that you'd welcome me with open arms,'
Barry said warmly, then coughed delicately at her glare.
'Um, could I come in out of the wind and discuss this
with you in a pseudo-rational and semi-civilised
manner?'

Sara backed up ungraciously, muttering under her
breath, 'I'm feeling about as rational as an avocado,' to
which Barry choked out a laugh that immediately died
when she looked at him so fiercely that he fell back a
pace. She was for the most part a very mild person, but
when she lost her temper she was like a tornado bent on
destruction. She was not, Barry ascertained uneasily, in
the best of moods at the moment. The situation might
get touchy.

'You didn't answer me, Barry,' Sara repeated grimly.
'What do you think you're doing here? I'll give you five
minutes—which is more than you deserve, I might
say—and then you get thrown out, so you'd better start
talking fast!'

'Would you really?' he asked, intrigued in spite of
himself. She didn't bother to reply but merely sat down
on the couch and looked at him with those large,
determined eyes. He stared at her, assessing her
expression, taking in the slight tilt to the jaw and the
firmly held mouth. She would, he decided. He sat too,
at one end of the couch, and regarded her warily.

He was almost impossibly thin and tall, with a habit
of moving jerkily and talking fast. His sandy hair fell
into his eyes continually and one of his nervous
mannerisms was pushing it off his forehead with his left
hand with a flick of his first two fingers. He did so now,
as he stared at her with his light blue eyes.

'Elise was wondering how you're doing,' he began,
and Sara abruptly threw her head back and laughed.

'And you came halfway across the continent to tell me

that! I'm so touched! Come on, Barry, you're wasting your time. Spill it!' she ordered tersely. 'Why have you come when I expressly told you that I didn't want to see, hear, think, or otherwise be reminded of yours or anyone else's presence from California until I gave you word? You fool, don't you realise that your arrival here could trigger off just exactly the kind of interest that I don't need right now? What if the press got word of me staying here? You know they've followed you in the past. You could have destroyed this vacation, and if you have I'll never forgive you! God, my first vacation in years!' she ended disgustedly, shooting poison darts at him with her eyes.

He was watching her with a reluctant admiration. She was very beautiful when she was angry, with her large hazel eyes spitting brimstone, and her face vivid, animated. 'I had a time tracking you down,' he admitted. 'Then Elise dragged out of her memory the name Three Oaks, and from there it was relatively easy. I called around the area and found a certain Sara Carmichael in residence, so I got the first flight out. What a godforsaken spot!'

'Watch it!' he was warned sternly. 'So, now I know how, but you haven't yet told me why?'

'You are going to flip, absolutely flip,' he told her, satisfaction oozing from every thin, awkward line of his body. She had to smile at that, reluctantly.

'I think I could "flip" right now,' she told him dryly, 'and it's not a favourable reaction at the moment.'

'Yes, well,' he put in hurriedly, 'you'll love what I've got to say. Sara, we've been offered a chance to do a television special, to be broadcast nationwide! You wouldn't believe the monetary figures that they quoted to me, it would just about blow your mind, it——'

Sara was interested in spite of herself, feeling a thrill of excitement at the thought of her own television special. 'You have to be joking!'

'Babe, you are what is currently termed a "hot item"

at the moment. Everybody loves you and everybody wants you,' he said in a wordly tone of voice. It was dropped the next minute when he laughed delightedly. 'Can you believe it? Can you really believe it? I knew you were big-time, love, but this is a godsend—think of the publicity from that one night's viewing!'

Sara looked at Barry with amusement. Not only was this a high point in her career, but it was a high point in his also. She was his first major star, and his name would become very much in demand because of her success. His career as an agent was skyrocketing right along with hers. Feeling charged up, she stood suddenly and started to pace around the room with long quick strides (seven *up*, seven *back*, five to the *front* door . . .). She shook her head impatiently and turned to Barry once again. 'When do they want me to do it? she asked jerkily.

'They want you to start on it right away. If you could pack this afternoon, I could get you a flight back with me——'

'No way.' Her reply came out without any hesitation. He blinked. 'What?'

'I said no way. I'm on vacation, a long, leisurely, much dreamed of, badly needed vacation. No, I won't come back with you for any amount of money or publicity that this world could offer me,' she said calmly, and sat down to wait for the fall-out from the explosion that inevitably came.

It wasn't long in coming. Barry argued, pleaded, stormed about the room and nearly dissolved into tears, but she was adamant. Finally, after nearly an hour and a half of hot argument, he sank down on to the couch, defeated.

Sara was seated at the piano bench and leaning against the closed top. She couldn't help but laugh at his total dejection as he sprawled all over the cushions. She said, laughing, 'Look, Barry, if I'm such a hot item, as you so sophisticatedly put it, then I can afford to be exclusive, can't I? I can afford to pick and choose?'

'A television special,' he moaned into his hands. 'Goddamned prime time!' This made her laugh even harder.

'Can't you get them to wait until I get back from vacation? I want to do the programme, really——'

'—you could have fooled me!' he muttered, but she chose to ignore the interruption and went on.

'—but on my terms. I would like to do totally new songs, at my own discretion, except maybe a few of my best hits, which I'm sure they would insist upon, and I want to have the last say as to whom I work with. The money doesn't matter . . .' Barry moaned again, '. . . and I'll start only when I get back. Surely that wouldn't be too hard to work out, would it?'

'I don't know,' he said gloomily. 'It'll probably take months to come to an agreement.'

'Well, then,' she said serenely. He glowered at her from over one hand. Sara abandoned her relaxed position and stood suddenly to stare down at him with a fierce gleam in her eye. 'And I will not, repeat not, do the special at all if you so much as send me a picture postcard again while I'm here, do you hear? I mean it, Barry. I don't want even a phone call.'

He winced. 'Oh, I hear all right. Haven't a choice about it, do I? Can't I even drop you a line to let you know if they agree to your terms?'

She thought about it and then shrugged. 'All right, but only one letter. If I'm bothered outside that one letter, I won't come within a mile of signing a contract!'

They talked for some time more, then Sara led Barry gently but firmly to the front door and shoved him out, in spite of his protests. She leaned against the door, then did a happy little dance in the middle of the living room floor. Live concerts were really a potent charge emotionally, and concert tours were an excellent income source, but she could reach more people in one television special than she could in months of touring, though it might pay less. It was the chance of a lifetime, a chance that many big-named performers would give their eye teeth for, and it had dropped into her lap like a ripe plum.

She need not have any doubts about the quality of the special. If Barry could work out the creative terms that she had stipulated, then she could be on the verge of doing one of the best creative performances of her life. With the terms she had insisted on, she could indulge in whatever style of music caught her mood at the time. She was fairly sure that she could make her creative urges known in a style that would appeal to her audience, though it might differ from her past musical expression. And, she told herself gleefully, I still have my vacation.

Then she remembered Greg.

# CHAPTER FOUR

IT was dusk when Greg finally came over.

Sara answered the door almost immediately when he knocked, and she looked into a frowning face. 'Come in,' she invited, uncertainly. He crossed the threshold promptly, though, and she breathed an unconscious sigh of relief.

'You really should identify your caller before you so blithely open your door,' he said tersely, and looked at her with something close to accusation in his eyes. 'You didn't know that it was me just now, did you?'

She felt taken aback just now, attacked, and was at a loss for a reply. 'Yes, thank you, and I hope you had a nice afternoon too,' she finally murmured sarcastically. Her nerves were on edge. She had been keyed up all day, and had been through such a variety of emotions in a relatively short time, and to top it off, she had worried over her feelings for Greg like a dog with a juicy bone. She was not exactly in a calm state of mind.

Greg was glaring at her, however, and his mouth was held tight. A muscle moved in his square jaw and, staring at it, she decided to back down for now.

'Would you like some coffee?' she asked, taking a few steps to the kitchen with an enquiring look over her shoulder.

He declined the offer with a quick shake of the head. 'I just stopped by to let you know that I was outside. I'll go and look around for you now.' Something about the way he spoke, something about the harsh lines of his face and his tense glittering eyes made her react sharply, goaded.

'Please, don't go to any trouble on my account,' she

told him mockingly, hurt by his inexplicable attitude. Her self-effacing act stung him, she could tell, by his sudden stillness and quick jerk of the head.

'Stop it!' he said coldly. Those dark eyes, she saw, had that same repelling quality that they had contained the day before, and her heart sank at the observation. He had erected the wall again. He was blocking her out, right now. She hurt.

'Why should I?' She swung away from him and put some distance between them. It didn't make her feel any better. 'You're the one who came in here with a great big hostile chip on your shoulder about something! So I didn't answer my door the way you would like me to! I didn't ask for this kind of treatment, and frankly, if this is how you're going to act about merely looking around outside tonight, I'd rather you didn't!'

Something flickered in his expressionless face then. He put his back to her and rubbed his neck in a tired gesture. 'All right, I'm sorry. Look, it isn't you, it's me. I've—had a bad afternoon, that's all.' Sara stood still, fighting the urge to go and put her arms around his waist. It's too soon, she thought. I can't. We got too intense, for just a silly argument. Not yet—I'm too unsure. Greg turned and caught the look on her face and suddenly, jerkily as if he couldn't help himself, came and put his arms around her in a rough embrace. Her arms went around him as eagerly, and they just held each other tightly for a moment. Her head had just sank to his broad chest as she felt an overpowering wave of an unfamiliar emotion, and he jerked her away as abruptly as he had pulled her to him. He stared down into her eyes, holding her face with his two broad, calloused hands. She felt shocked; the depth of torment she saw in those brown eyes rocked her to the core. 'Look——' he started, then his lips came down on hers in a crushing kiss, quick and unsatisfying. 'I'll come around and see you tomorrow, okay?'

Sara's eyes were huge in her face. She didn't know what to feel, whether to feel hurt, anger or sympathy. This man tore up her emotions more than any other single human being. She whispered, 'Sure,' and thought dully, he's not coming back. He is not going to come.

Greg must have been able to read her thoughts on her confused face, for his softened slightly as he repeated, 'I will see you tomorrow, Sara, I promise.' Then he was gone, and she didn't feel any better after his last words than she had before. He shook her up so violently. She brooded all evening long.

All in all, she had completely forgotten to feel even a little nervous about the dark night, the empty house, and the memory of that tall black shape that moved in the night.

The ticking of the bedside clock was so loud to her that she nearly picked up the offending object to hurl it across her bedroom. It was close to three in the morning and she was still so tense that every muscle was held rigid, aching. And of course, the more she thought about it and fussed, the more rigid she became. She needed a cigarette; her nerves were a total wreck. She couldn't stop thinking and thinking. Everything that happened to her in the past few days came whirling back, like an old film being replayed over and over and being stopped at the best parts. She threw back her covers in disgust, too warm and so restless that the weight on her legs aggravated her more than anything else, or would have, except that everything else was aggravating her as much the stifling blankets. And so on and so forth, her mind chanted disgustedly.

The worst single problem was the quiet. The place was so damned quiet, like a tomb, and she couldn't rest in such quiet. She wanted someone to honk a blaring horn, she wanted the noise of downtown Los Angeles— no, she wanted—she didn't know what she wanted.

One, two, creak. That floorboard, she thought

vaguely, is going to drive me crazy one of these days—
she froze in sudden horror, the pit of her stomach just
dropping away into nothingness and her heart starting
to pound so hard that she thought it must surely burst
her chest apart. That creaking floorboard was in the
middle of her living room. It was such a totally
harmless sound, such a completely ordinary everyday
sound. Until you realised the context of the sound.

That creaking floorboard only creaked when someone
walked over it.

There was someone in her living room. There was an
actual, real, unimagined and unknown person at that
very moment creeping across her living room floor.

She was so totally, completely, utterly alone in the
house, in the dark, in that terrible silence. God, she
thought in a silent scream, *I can't move!* I'm going to be
killed in my bed, because I can't get my stupid asinine
body to move! Three, and a pause, and then four. Seven
steps across the open space in the living room, she
recalled suddenly, pulling the knowledge out of the
darkness like a magician pulling a rabbit out of the hat.
One corner of her brain registered this analogy with a
stunned incredulity. Seven steps and then the hall, and
my bedroom down here, so close, at the end of the hall
with the door wide open. Dear sweet heaven, why did I
ever leave the door open? But the question was
academic and she knew it. There was no reason for her
to shut her bedroom door if she lived alone.

Sweat poured off her body and she shook as if she
had a chill. The so quiet steps and the silent night made
her want to scream in a mad orgy of hysteria. The
horror and the terrible fear almost held her bound to
the bed with the crazy desire to go to sleep, to wake and
to know that she was dreaming. She wanted to pull the
covers over head and feel safe, as if she were a little
child hiding from the shadows of the outside night.

*Five!*

The tiny shuffle of sound that she would have never heard had she been asleep shrieked through her head and she nearly moaned. That one sound had ruined irreparably the illusion that she might have possibly imagined the whole thing after all. Isolation. Rape. Death—oh, *God*!

After being unable to move for what had seemed a thousand eternities, she suddenly found herself standing by the bed without ever having realised that she had moved after all. Frozen there like a silent wraith, she played over in her mind the remembrance, the echo of creaking bedsprings that had accompanied her rise, and with sudden urgent, shaking hands, she reached down and gently pushed the bed down. The bed creaked again, as if she had rolled over in her sleep. The utter terrible silence that came from the living room told her that whoever it was had frozen and was listening intently.

She nearly turned on the light and called out to the unknown person. The crazy desire to give herself up and see once and for all who was down the hall was almost her undoing. Then she shook herself violently and thought with a goading desperation. I have to get out of here! I have to run. Where? Where can I go?

The answer was like a sigh. Greg. Without another second's hesitation, she silently scooped up her dressing gown that was at the foot of her bed and her shoes on the floor. She slid to the window to look frantically at its latch. The feeling of entrapment, of utter helplessness, of blinding fear was gagging her at the base of the throat.

Six. She heard that footstep and nearly threw up. Then something clicked in her head like a computer terminal coming on, and her brain was racing faster than it had ever in her life.

She had a very slight advantage. She was at the end of the hall and whoever it was in the living room was almost certainly unaware of the floor plan of the house. He might have a good idea of where her bedroom was, but he wouldn't know for sure, and the same necessity for quiet that was hampering her movements was hampering his. If he still thought she was asleep. But at that, she shook her head and was totally unaware of the movement. The silence throughout the house told her that he still thought she was asleep.

The window latch was a simple turn lock, and the window one that swung out on a hinge. She could have wept from relief at the merciful God that had ordained such a simple style of window, for it excluded the possibility of a windowscreen, an obstacle that would have trapped her like iron bars in a prison. She slid her hand to the latch and carefully, oh, so carefully, began to turn it. Her hands were shaking so violently that she was barely able to grasp the handle with her nerveless fingers, but she soon saw the latch come free of its rest.

Seven. He was at the hall opening. Was it about twenty feet away, or thirty? If the window creaked when she pushed it open, he would hear it as clearly as a gunshot. He would down the hall in two seconds flat. The fear in Sara's mouth made her tongue stick to the roof with its dryness. She nearly fainted when she pushed the window out on its hinges.

It went as silently and as smoothly as the quiet stalk of a panther.

Sara was small and she was out of that window opening in a split second, pausing only to push the window shut again in an attempt to fool the intruder, then she was tiptoeing around the corner of the house, completely unaware of the sharp sticks that bit into the bottom of her soft feet. She hit the beginning of the path that lead to the beach at a dead run.

Of course she fell. That funny hitch in the path that was caused by tree roots caught her toes and she pitched headlong into the darkness, to fall bruisingly.

Sheer unadulterated panic was gripping her by the throat, though, and she was up and running almost before she could breathe.

Never had the trip to the beach seemed so long and frighteningly black. He was behind her, she knew, with hands like claws almost to her throat, her hair, dragging her back along the path to that silent house. She kicked up sand as she sprinted, her breath coming in huge agonising gasps. It wasn't really happening after all. It couldn't be!

She faltered at the rise only for a second and then scrabbled up frantically, feeling the cold bitter wind bite through her flimsy nightdress. It was as if she really didn't have anything on. She was completely unaware of the dressing gown and shoes that she still clutched in a death-grip. Her feet were ice and totally deadened to sensation. She was down the other side of the rise and stumbling along the beach with an iron band around her chest and her hair whipped around her neck.

It was here that the tears started to fall, for she was in fear's control, and it was very dark with little moonlight to show the way. She wasn't sure where the path was that lead to Greg's house. The murmur of the waves behind her was like a scream of rage, and the gentle wind rustling the undergrowth was a thousand night stalkers, her death on their minds.

Eternity came and went when she finally found the path and stumbled along it. Little animal-like moans startled her, even more so when she found that they were coming from her own throat. Something black loomed ahead, and she barely paused to ascertain where the door in the silent structure was before she fell on it, pounding frantically and bruising her wrists. She never felt a thing.

It was terrible, standing at the closed door and begging to be let in while she had at her back the black, silent, infinitely menacing forest. He was going to be too late, she knew, she just knew, for the unknown

assailant was right behind her, he was about to grab her
and kill her horribly—and a thought struck her, as she
stood leaning against the door with her cheek pressed to
it. 'Oh, dear Lord,' she groaned. Don't let it be Greg.
Please, don't let it be him. Please!

The door was jerked violently open and she fell into
Greg's arms, sobbing wildly.

She heard above her head an uttered ejaculation, and
he exclaimed profoundly shocked, 'Sara! Dammit,
what's happened? Are you hurt? Are you all right?
Oh—hellfire!' This last was accompanied by a shove of
the foot to the open door, and the hard arms that had
closed around her so tightly loosened. Sara moaned
deep in her throat and clung to him, shaking like a leaf,
but he was only flipping on a light switch and his arms
came back around her, reassuringly firm. He held her to
his body heat when he realised that she was as cold as
ice. She didn't protest; she couldn't have stood alone if
she tried. Her head was bent to his wide chest and she
was heaving in great gulps of air in an effort to catch
her breath after her headlong dash across the beach. It
wasn't easy, since she was trying to talk and cry at the
same time, with every gulp.

Greg took one look at her saucer-like eyes, dilated
pupils, pinched white face and thinly clad body, and
bent to pick her up, one arm to her shoulders and one
beneath her knees. Her two hands were entwined in
what she now saw to be a black dressing robe, loosely
belted at the waist. She never let go, as he walked down
a length of hall to what opened into a spaciously large
den, thickly carpeted, with a huge fireplace. He
deposited her carefully on a couch, then found that he
couldn't stand up because of her knuckle-clenched hold
on his dressing gown's lapel. He sat immediately, his
own hands coming up to hers to try and gently pry her
loose. Failing that, he merely stroked the backs of those
thin cold hands soothingly. They were trembling.

She couldn't see him through the sudden moisture in her eyes, and finally got a hold on herself enough to let go with one hand and knuckle her eyes. 'S-sorry,' she whispered, teeth chattering. 'Sorry to bother you. I didn't mean to wake you up, it's just that I—God, I can't——'

A warm hand came up to rub at her cheek roughly, the thumb stroking her lips over and over. 'Shh! Get a grip of yourself, Sara. Calm down a bit first ... hold on, now, you're safe. Calm down—that's it.' He talked this way until he saw a measure of rationality come back into her eyes, replacing that blind, unreasoning panic of a few minutes before.

Her eyes cleared, and she could see him, hair tousled and face hard and the eyes so concerned that she nearly started to cry again, but caught herself up in time. He asked softly, 'Better now?' and she nodded a quick jerk of the head. 'Perhaps you can tell me about it, then?'

The words tumbled out about the seven steps in the living room and the creaky floorboard and that she didn't shut her bedroom door and the tree roots that she stumbled over and the whole thing had started when she couldn't sleep. Greg's face showed incomprehension.

'Sara, honey, maybe it's because I've just woken up, but I don't seem to understand a word ...' He paused and his face whitened, and his hand at her cheek slid to her collarbone to tighten convulsively, making her wince. Then he was speaking in such a harsh voice that she couldn't believe that it came from the same person. 'Someone broke into your house? Tonight—just now? Someone was in your house?' She nodded, and he seemed to hesitate, with a strangely sick fear in his eyes. Then, 'Did he hurt you, Sara?'

She shook her head dumbly, sniffing a little. His dark eyes travelled over her stained nightgown and bare legs, took in the bruised and bleeding feet, the slender fingers nearly blue with cold, the trembling lips. He then saw for the first time the crumpled dressing gown on the floor and the small pair of shoes tumbled beside it. She saw his face become expressionless, then realised that his eyes had turned nearly black with a molten rage. He was nearly choking her and didn't seem to realise it and she croaked, 'Please, your hand!'

She was loosened immediately, and Greg stood up in one lithe upsurging motion. If she had thought he had looked dangerous before tonight, she hadn't seen anything to compare with the murderous look in his eyes and the taut, jerking line of his jaw muscle. His big hands were clenched with the bones showing white and his body was held like a weapon. When he turned on his heel and simply left the room, she was left feeling nonplussed. Whatever she had expected from him, it hadn't been that.

After a minute, she stood and followed him, wincing at the throb from her bruised feet. Being alone in the den made her nervous. She followed the hall to a stairway and uncertainly climbed the stairs. At the top, she found a light streaming from an open door and, approaching hesitantly, she saw Greg pulling jeans over brief undershorts. His bare body looked very powerful, the chest muscles and flat stomach gleaming in the yellow golden light thrown by the bedside lamp. His face was like granite. After the jeans came a thick pullover sweater, and he drew that on, shoulder muscles flexing. Sara watched with a growing perplexity and fear. It didn't even occur to her to be embarrassed by his naked body; she was too overwhelmed with the problems of the moment to notice.

'What are you doing?' The question came out in a whisper, but he heard and turned, his dark head moving in a neat swift movement.

'Getting dressed; what does it look like?' He was

terse, angry. He was angry with her. She crossed her arms over her chest in a defensive gesture, her face flooding with unhappiness. The whole thing was just such a nightmare. Greg crossed over to her and passed his hand over her hair swiftly, his face gentling as he saw her distress. 'I'm going to your house.'

'*No!*' she burst out, clutching his arms before he withdrew. 'You can't! What if—what if he's still there?'

His dark eyes mocked her gently. He seemed almost calm. That was why his words were so shocking to her. 'Then I think I might kill him.'

The shock stayed with her until he had sat down on the edge of the bed to pull on socks and shoes, and then she erupted in a wild babble of incoherency. 'Greg, it's insane, you can't ... you could get hurt, killed—oh, please, promise me you won't go until tomorrow, no, you mustn't leave me ...' Then, as he bent to pick up his jacket, she cried out, *'Greg, don't leave me here alone!'*

That sank in. His head jerked and he stared at her with his eyes widened, taking in her tangible fear, the shadows behind her, the quiet house. He hesitated, then came over to her. 'You'd be all right here with Beowulf. Nothing could happen to you.'

'What about you?' Her eyes searched his face. 'Please, if you go, then I want to go, too. I—Greg, I can't stay here alone!'

'I know,' he soothed, then hesitated. 'I know. Come on, let's go get your dressing gown and shoes. You're not going back barefoot.'

Sara didn't know whether to feel weak from relief that she wasn't staying in a strange house alone or whether to feel sick from the fear of going out into that dark night again. After she had slipped on her shoes and dressing gown, he turned off the lights and put an arm around her shoulders as he opened the door for them to go out on to the porch. Beowulf slipped out of the door and then Greg was locking it. All too soon they were back on the path that would take them to Sara's house and, as if he knew just what she was feeling, Greg put his arm around her, holding her firmly to his side. He didn't let her go until they reached the end of the path, then he whispered in her ear, 'Stay here a minute.' She barely had time for a nod before he was slipping away, melting into the night like a shadow.

What would he find? What if he was attacked? She knelt and found a thick stick by the path and was after him before she let her fear conquer her. She came up behind him just as he reached the porch and gently touched his arm. He whirled, incredibly fast, with arm up and fist clenched, checking only when he saw it was her. He took in her wary stance, and the stick in her hand before she felt a hand plucking it wryly away. The moonlight was shining enough for her to see his dark shape, bulky, strong, reassuring, in front of her. He was hefting the stick thoughtfully. He kept it in one hand and held her behind him with the other. In this way they crept to the dark rectangle that was her front door. It looked so alien in the dark. She couldn't have recognised it if she had been on her own.

A silent push of the foot had the door swinging gently open. She put a hand over her mouth to stifle any noise she might make. Greg pushed her against the outside wall and warned her with the hard pressure of his hand to stay there. Then he crashed inside, flipping the light switch by the side of the door and moving swiftly. There was silence, and she couldn't stand it, so she came in too, her eyes darting around the empty room.

Greg had disappeared and she followed him quickly down the hall to the light shining from her bedroom. He was standing in the middle of the floor, swinging the stick thoughtfully against his thigh as he looked around at the wreckage of the room. He turned at the sound of her footsteps. 'The light was left on, Sara, I'm sorry about the——'

Whatever else he said rushed away in the roaring that filled her ears as she took in the ruined furniture, the clothes strewn about. A reeking odour told her that her favourite bottle of perfume had been smashed, and the sense of violation at this invasion of her privacy was so intense that she swayed dizzily against the doorpost.

Greg was very quick. He was at her side in a split second, putting his arms around her and supporting her, hiding the room from her gaze. It was nice to be held and rocked so gently and easily. After a minute she opened her eyes and stared into his dark intent gaze. He rubbed her cheek. 'Okay now?'

'I think so. Sorry about being so stupid.' She was shaky when she stood back from him, but he kept his arm around her waist until she sat carefully on the bed.

His face crinkled into a smile. 'If you don't stop saying you're sorry, I may get violent!'

Sara laughed shakily, appreciating his effort. 'Sorry.' He growled.

As she looked around, the mess all over the floor brought the same fear back again, and her mouth shook when she saw her favourite blouse thrown into the corner, ripped in two. When she looked back at Greg, her eyes reflected her hurt and fear and vulnerability. 'Why?' she whispered. 'Why me? Why would someone want to do this? I don't understand it.' She bent and picked up a broken piece of ceramic near her ankle. It had been a hand-painted vase, picked up in Mexico along with the coffee mugs. She said a little forlornly, 'It was my favourite piece, too.'

Greg knelt at her side and looked for the other pieces, finding four altogether. He concentrated briefly and looked up with an encouraging smile. 'Maybe we can glue them together again. See, it didn't shatter, and the jagged edges fit together perfectly.'

Seeing him at her feet, eager to comfort and reassure after being so intense and huge and violent, made her smile involuntarily. 'We'll try.' His hand came up and gripped her a moment, then fell away as he stood up briskly. A trip to her half open closet had him pulling out a suitcase and dumping it on the bed. She watched, eyes huge in her exhausted face. He started to pull out clothes that were still hanging up, dumping them in the open suitcase. 'What are you doing?'

He grinned. 'Favourite question for the evening, is it? I'm packing for you, sweet Sara-Sue. You're going to come home with me.'

She didn't feel guilt or embarrassment at this, perhaps because she was so tired. Instead, she felt suffused with an intense relief. 'Oh,' she sighed, 'can I?' It earned her a quick kiss on the forehead.

'Just try and stop it.' Greg looked around the room assessingly, and a slightly puzzled expression puckered his eyes. 'How did you manage to get out of the house, if you were all the way down at this end of the hall, and the front and back doors at the other end of the house?'

She stood and went to the window, pulling back the curtains to show him the unlatched side. 'I was lucky. There wasn't a screen on the window, and I just slipped outside.' With a finger, she showed how easily and silently it swung open, then she closed and latched it again with a shudder.

Greg had watched her with a frown. 'Well,' he muttered, 'that's something we can thank your landlord for, although normally I'd chew him out for not properly covering the windows. Funny, isn't it?' He ran an eye quickly down her, and she looked down at herself at that. The dressing gown looked dirty, and the bedraggled nightdress peeped out from underneath. 'You might like to put on jeans or something until we get back. It looks like your nightgown has just about had it for the night.'

She chuckled wryly. 'I see what you mean. It's so cold out, I'd appreciate something warmer, anyway.'

He was walking towards the door and paused. 'How long do you think it will take you to finish packing?'

Sara glanced at the mess he had made of things. 'Maybe fifteen minutes?'

'I'm going to check out the rest of the house while you dress and pack. Don't shut the door all the way, all right? Yell if you need anything. I'll be just a call away.'

A call away. It sounded nice. She gave him a sweet smile before he left, causing him to stop and stare at her with an unreadable expression. She turned and, shivering slightly, twitched the curtains closed, blocking out that black night. Alone, she quickly dragged on a pair of jeans and a sweater. Rummaging around on the floor, she managed to locate her brush, and a few flicks through her hair took care of the tangles whipped in it from the wind. Then she set about finding underwear and night-clothes that weren't saturated with perfume, stuffing them into one side of the suitcase. She then straightened the clothes that Greg had thrown in, adding the rest of the undamaged things. After that, she walked down the hall in search of her purse. It was where she had left it, in the hall cupboard at the bottom, with the linen. Out of curiosity she rummaged through her wallet with a puzzled frown. A step sounded behind her and she jumped before realising that it was only Greg returning from the garage. He surveyed her kneeling posture. 'Anything missing?'

She shook her head slowly. 'No. All the cash I had is still here, and my identification. See, even my lip gloss . . . no, everything is untouched.' She held the things in both hands and looked up with eyes that didn't see him. 'What do you suppose he wanted?'

'Your car is still in the garage. I think we'd better drive it over to my place just in case.' Beowulf came panting up and bumped Greg's knee, and he reached down to rub the dog's head absently. 'There's room in my garage.' His gaze sharpened on her. 'Stop it, Sara! He didn't really have time to steal anything. We got here too quickly for that; in fact, we probably scared him away. Sara?' Her eyes focussed on him. 'You're safe, I promise. Okay?' At her nod, he said bracingly, 'Good girl. Are you packed?'

'I need my things from the bathroom,' she replied tiredly. 'I'll go and put them in my handbag.' Greg was trying to make her feel better, but all the same, she would have felt a little better if the unknown intruder had at least taken her handbag. He had taken the time to rip her room apart, surely he could have taken the time to look into cupboards if he had been a thief. Her handbag had not been hidden, merely put away. But she knew deep down that the intruder had not been a thief. He had known that she was home, and it would not be hard to find out that she lived alone. No thief would want to take the chance of getting caught by the house's occupants; they would wait until the occupants were gone before attempting to rob a place. That was what scared her, and Greg knew it.

She had given him her car keys before going into the bathroom and getting her toothbrush, cleansing cream and cosmetics, stuffing them haphazardly into the recesses of her handbag. Then she went back into the living room and sat quietly on the couch until Greg came back into the house. He passed by her, however, and soon emerged from her bedroom with a leather jacket in his hands.

'You'll need this. It's getting cold.' She stood and he helped her into it and then, turning out all of the lights and whistling for Beowulf, he led her out of the house. Sara saw a quick sharp glance from him, in the light of the car's headlights. 'Do you mind if I drive?'

At that she grimaced at him. 'I'd prefer it, the way I feel now. I feel just like a zombie!'

A guiding hand helped her into the passenger seat as he said quietly, 'You've just about had it, I think. It's been an unsettling day for such a little girl.'

She chuckled at the gentle mocking tone. At the moment she felt like a small child being helped by an older brother, and the feeling was safe and pleasant. She leaned back in the bucket seat and drowsily perused the profile of the man beside her. He was so hard and yet so gentle. With a flash of perception she realised that he was probably acting like an older brother on purpose. He had sensed that she was close to the end of her tether.

Beowulf panted heavily in the small back seat, sprawled all over her suitcase and handbag. She glanced back, grinning at his wicked white smile and long tongue. A faint whine and wag of the tail was his response.

They were very soon pulling into the long winding drive that cut into Greg's property, and when he smoothly pulled the car to a stop and got out, Sara slid across the seat to sit in the driver's position. Greg went on into the house to open the garage door. Beowulf waited patiently in the back of the car. A few moments passed and then the long rectangular garage door slid silently up to reveal an empty parking place beside an expensive model sports car.

She changed gears and quickly pulled her car into the parking position and switched off the engine. Greg was there before the purr of the car's motor had ceased, opening the door and helping her out. He reached in the back and hauled out her suitcase after Beowulf had bounded out.

Sara was reeling on her feet from exhaustion. She guessed fuzzily that it must be around five in the morning or so, and a wave of weary anger shook through her when she thought of the unknown intruder who had disrupted her placid life and had caused her so much personal anguish. 'Damn him!' she muttered half-tearfully. 'Damn him to hell!'

A guiding hand propelled her forward, into the adjoining house, and she was vaguely aware of the dark brown hues of the den passing by, the stairs negotiated with considerable help from Greg, and then at some indeterminate distance down the second storey hallway a bedroom with a soft warm bed. That was all she noticed. As soon as Greg had turned on the light, she headed for that bed. Without a murmur she sank on to the bedspread and was out as soon as her head hit the downy pillow. She never felt the gentle hands that undressed her as if she were a baby, pulling a loose nightgown over her unconscious head and tucking her underneath the covers as lovingly as any mother. She never realised the care with which her head was arranged on the pillow, and she never felt the hand that stroked her dark cloudy mane of hair before Greg removed himself and turned out the light. He left the door open and Beowulf snoozed at the foot of the bed.

Sara moaned and rolled over in bed. Her eyes flew open as she felt how extraordinarily sore she was in certain areas, and her misty gaze travelled wonderingly over strange walls and furniture. A puzzled smile touched her lips as she vaguely wondered if she was still dreaming, and then the events of last night came tumbling back into her consciousness and she bolted up in bed like a rabbit breaking from cover. Beowulf raised his black head and thumped his stump at her. Funny, she thought, frowning, I don't remember undressing. She put up a hand and scratched at her ribcage at a slight discomfort and found that she was still wearing her bra. She never wore a bra to bed and rarely wore one when she took a nap, it was so uncomfortable. But then, she acknowledged wryly, she never ran down a beach in a nightgown and got a man out of bed at three in the morning before, either. She dismissed the whole train of thought as being unimportant, since she didn't remember entering this strange bedroom last night anyway. Actually, it was early this morning, but who was counting?

She gingerly edged her feet off the bed and stood, wincing at the pain from her feet. A quick inspection showed them to be lacerated and bruised. A black mark was on her left ankle. A quick exploration of the room revealed a small bath off to the left, and she went into it with an anticipatory gleam in her eye. She was prevented from shutting the door behind her, however, by a quick powerful shove from a waist-high canine head. Beowulf watched her with velvet eyes.

'Oh, all right!' she told him laughingly, and let him in to plop on the tiled floor. 'I'll have you know, young man, that you're the first male that I've ever let into my bathroom!' He looked duly appreciative of that fact, then rolled over on to his side with a snort. He was still there when she emerged from the shower stall some time later. She had found several more bruises all over her body and whenever she moved unwarily she felt painful twinges that warned her to be careful. It had hurt, standing in the shower and having the warm soapy water lap at her feet, but she knew that at least it had cleaned out the cuts.

She dressed for comfort in the pair of jeans that she had donned around four in the morning, and a red long-sleeved blouse. It helped hide her bruises. Then she brushed her long black hair with the hand dryer that she'd packed until her hair was moderately dry. Make-up? It was out of the question; she felt strangely exhausted at the effort that she had expended already. All she managed to do to her feet was pull a thick pair of cushiony socks on. She had tried shoes and found they hurt too much.

Beowulf accompanied her every move, even to sitting with his great head on her knee as she blow-dried her hair. He was comic and adorable, and by the time she had finished with her laborious toilet, she had fallen into the habit of talking aloud to him. It was uncanny how he managed to respond appropriately to various spoken statements.

Sara was soon heading out of her bedroom door and attempting to limp down the stairs when Greg appeared with a coffee mug in hand and several papers in the other. He immediately put them on a side table and jumped up the stairs when he took in her involuntary winces of pain. He reached out, and she felt his hands take hold of her in a firm grip, then the world swung around as he hauled her up in his arms to carry her down the rest of the stairs.

She felt shy and awkward. All of the reactions from last night that she normally would have felt but had been too upset to bother with came rushing up. She remembered Greg's bare muscular body as he had angrily shrugged into his jeans and sweater from last night, and her face burned. She felt the natural embarrassment for putting someone out, someone that she hardly knew. It coloured her voice.

'Good morning,' she began, but was cut short.

'Honey child, it's hardly morning,' he told her, amusement threading his voice. 'In fact it's well into the afternoon.'

Her face, already flushed, turned even more red. 'I'm sorry——'

Greg stopped in the middle of the hall, with Beowulf behind him, half on and half off the bottom of the stairs. His dark gaze caressed her. 'Don't start that again, Sara. I've had enough humility and contrite embarrassment to last me a long time!'

Her eyes twinkled tentatively. 'All right.' Greg resumed walking down the hall and Beowulf was able to finish coming down the stairs. Neither had noticed him.

She was asked, 'Are you feeling hungry?' to which she responded with a nod. 'Good! How about keeping me company in the kitchen while I fix us something to gobble?'

'Please.' He put her down on a bar stool beside a butcher block table and she soon had a steaming cup of coffee in front of her to nurse while he moved efficiently around the kitchen. Sara swung from side to side in an effort to see the stove clock, but with Greg moving around so much she couldn't see the time.

He caught her movement out of the corner of one eye and turned to contemplate her sardonically. 'Practising to become a pendulum some day?'

She chuckled. 'I'm trying to see what time it is. I have this very nagging desire to see how much of the day I've missed.' He obligingly moved out of the way, and she yelped. It was two-thirty in the afternoon.

'Want to lay odds on whether you'll be sleepy or not around ten this evening?' Greg asked her with a crooked smile.

She hesitated. 'N-no. It was hard enough to get out of bed just now. I think I'll be only too ready for bed tonight.'

He reached out for her cheek in a quick caress. It was an absentminded gesture, but it still sent a thrill through her. 'You went through a lot last night.' Her eyes slid away from his and she watched tiny motes of dust dance along a yellow sunbeam that peeped through a curtained window. 'Hey,' he said, 'cut it out. Don't think about it now, d'you hear?'

'Okay.' It was an empty promise, though, and they both knew it.

'What do you want to eat?' Greg was perusing the contents of his refrigerator, head cocked and foot tapping slowly.

'What have you got?' Sara's stomach was beginning to make sharp demands and she rubbed it unobtrusively.

'Does an onion and mushroom omelette sound good to you?'

'It sounds wonderful,' she sighed. 'Can we eat it now and cook it later, to save time?' His dark eyes laughed at her as he juggled items to the table. She watched while he chopped the mushrooms and laughed when her eyes watered as he peeled the onion. The aroma of eggs nicely browning in butter made her mouth salivate. When he slid a steaming plate of food her way, she tucked in with a neat concise eagerness that made him smile to himself. He sat across from her. After they had finished their meal, he stood and fed Beowulf, who swiftly gobbled his portion of dog food with an avidness that made her ask Greg if he had been starving the poor hound.

'It's the second time he's been fed today,' he replied dryly, crossing his arms and leaning against the doorway. 'That "poor hound" gets fed three times a day. I don't think he's hurting any.' Looking at Beowulf's sleek shiny coat and firm rippling muscles, Sara had to agree. He looked trim and fit, but he certainly didn't look thin or weak from lack of food.

Greg poured her another cup of coffee, and they lounged in the kitchen without saying much. It was a perfect opportunity for her to study him in depth. She was genuinely puzzled.

The barrier, so obvious yesterday evening and the first time she had met him, was missing today. He was showing himself to be a warm, compassionate man, sensitive to her needs and caring about her. His eyes were warm and sparkling, not hard and repelling. His face was still hard; nothing could soften those features after a point, but his expression was relaxed and easy, not wary and guarded.

He was an enigma. He was tantalising and unknown. In many ways he was a contradiction in terms. She couldn't get her mind off him. There was a power of being about him that manifested itself in certain ways: in the hard line of his jaw, in odd inflexibilities of his speech, in his quicksilver intelligence that forced her mind into a high gear of thought, in his quiet self-confidence. After a prolonged study of the lines of his face, Sara realised that he was like steel tempered by fire. The lines were not from maturity in years, but rather from suffering and hardship. She guessed that he had been through some kind of hell, and very probably was still dwelling in a private prison of damnation.

By the end of the afternoon, she had come to think of him as being beautiful, and she watched for every change in his mobile face, every different expression. He soon picked her up and carried her off to the downstairs bathroom, plunking her down decisively on the stool. She was laughing breathlessly, her hair all over her face, and she asked him with a mock sternness in her voice that was betrayed by a slight quiver, 'Just what do you think you're doing? If you think I'm going to go to the bathroom with you in here, you've got another think coming, buster! Beowulf's just the same. He insisted on coming into the bathroom with me when I took my shower.'

Greg knelt at her feet with a smile tugging at the corners of his lips and started to remove her socks. 'I'm going to have a look at the bottoms of your feet. I should have done this last night, but you were out like a light as soon as you hit the bed, and I didn't have the heart to disturb you.' He turned one small foot over gently and studied her bruises and lacerations.

It looked very small and white, held like that in his big-boned, darkly tanned hands. The delicate arch of her foot was mottled with black bruises and red cuts.

Sara wasn't thinking about her foot, though. She was still mulling over Greg's words. It must mean, she thought, with a squirm and a sudden rush of red, that he put me to bed last night. No wonder I didn't remember changing into my nightgown! His dark head came up and he sent her a slanting, mocking glance as if he knew what she was thinking. She said hurriedly, 'I made sure they were clean when I took my shower.'

'That must have hurt. I think we would be wise to put some antiseptic on those lacerations, just in case, since we left them a while before checking. Besides, I'd like to wrap them in gauze bandaging to keep them clean. That way you won't stick to your socks by the time you get ready for bed.' He turned, opened a small cabinet, and took out a first aid kit and soon was applying antiseptic to her feet. It made her eyes water from pain in spite of his obvious attempts to be gentle, and she took in a shaky breath when he finished one foot and wrapped it several times before sliding it back into her sock. By the end of the second foot she was gripping the edge of the sink and holding her lips so tightly that there was a white line around them.

Looking up, he caught sight of her pain, and took her unhesitatingly into his arms. The onrush of warmth from his caring and sympathy had her clinging to him with something akin to desperation. It felt so safe. He drew in a breath, looked down at her face so close to his own, and brought down his mouth. He was warm and his lips were firm and yet mobile. It shook her. He brushed her mouth over and over, then deepened the kiss with a gentle persuasion that had her responding almost before she realised it.

Afterwards, he helped her into the den, and Sara knew without any words being spoken that he had retreated once again.

# CHAPTER FIVE

GREG was very thoughtful. Sara was made comfortable and he brought her a paperback to read, and she had never felt so alone before in her life when he closed the door to his study after explaining that he needed to do some work.

Some time later she knocked softly on his door softly and was rewarded with an immediate and rather short, 'Come in.' She poked her head around the edge of the door after opening it halfway and Greg leaned back in his swivel chair, gesturing impatiently. 'I said come in, not peep at me like a mouse!'

So she limped in and leaned against the back of the chair in front of his desk to take the weight off her feet. 'I'm going back to the house now,' she began, and paused, and Greg came forward out of his chair with a resounding crash. It was quite an effective silencer and it had her staring at him with wide eyes.

'Like hell you are!' he shouted furiously. 'You've got to be crazy to even contemplate staying there after what happened! No way, lady, you are going to stay right here!'

She cocked an eyebrow, attempting to hide the flush of anger that suffused her mind. It had been a good eight years since anyone had dared to talk to her like that. Her mother was the last, and it had been a decade since she had heeded anything delivered to her in that tone of voice. She wasn't about to stand for it now, not from Greg or anyone else for that matter. 'Thank you for hearing me out,' she said sarcastically. The biting edge to her voice was keen. She knew her own voice intimately; she had to, to perform as well as she did.

She used her voice inflections to advantage now, and she saw him wince slightly. 'But I was about to finish with "pick up a few things." Now that you mention it, though, I might add another thank you for your kind hospitality last night, but I really must be going.' With that statement, she closed her mouth in what she knew to be an infuriating manner, turned her back on Greg, and limped with dignity out of the room. He caught up with her faster than she had expected.

She was whirled around and pushed against the nearby wall, imprisoned with two strong arms one to each side. Incensed with his cavalier manner, she brought up a stiff warning forefinger to stick it in front of his nose with a hiss through bared teeth, 'Watch it!'

He ignored the finger hovering near his nose. 'Where are you going?' It was a harsh tone of voice, one that she resented like she resented his attitude.

She answered him snappily, 'I'll let you know when I decide!' He was very big, she realised suddenly. His lower body was leaning against hers to keep her in place, and she found it quite distracting.

'Are you wanting to check into a motel, or are you going to go home?' he insisted, a thread of urgency colouring his question.

Sara's eyes dropped with a suffusion of doubt, and something in his face made her answer him seriously, 'I don't know, really. I hadn't thought about it.' With a quick sideways look up at his shadowed expression, she admitted tersely, 'You made me very angry.'

'I know,' he responded absently, 'Sara, don't feel you have to go home just because of this. Don't cut your vacation short. You can stay here if you like, for as long as you want. You'd be safe. Even if I needed to leave the house for a while, Beowulf is here and he would protect you.'

She stared at his shirt front, longing to stay so badly that she could taste it in her mouth. Uncertainties were undermining her thinking, though, and she couldn't seem to come to any rational decision. 'What—what about your privacy? I'd be an imposition, I'd upset your routine, I'd . . .'

He interrupted. 'You wouldn't be an imposition. Sara, do you want to stay?' An insistent hand was forcing her chin up, compelling her to look into his very serious eyes. She did so and found she couldn't look away.

'Yes.' It was a bare thread of sound, but he heard it anyway.

He said in a low voice, 'Then stay.' It was most persuasive, the intent and almost pleading way he spoke.

Sara closed her eyes and nodded.

Greg didn't accompany her back to the house since he had several things that he needed to do, but he insisted that she take Beowulf with her and let him run through the cabin before she entered. It was a good suggestion, and she accepted gratefully.

He told her not to be surprised if she found items in the house moved around a little. 'I took the liberty of calling the police this morning while you were in bed,' he explained, 'and they went through the house to check for fingerprints, but didn't find any. Whoever it was had to be wearing gloves. They also determined his mode of entry. He'd picked the lock, I guess.'

The front door swung open silently and the house loomed so quiet and empty in front of her that she was more than happy to let the huge dog bound ahead and sniff out the place. While he disappeared, she inspected the front lock like Greg had suggested, and noticed the scratch marks around the lock. It was immensely frightening, those small, telltale marks.

Beowulf was trotting back into the living room easily, his demeanour placid, so she went in and locked the door behind her, only afterwards realising how futile that really was. She had a competent guard dog with her, though, and she felt more or less at ease. Even so she didn't want to waste time.

She went straight to the phone and dialled long-distance to California, and soon she heard Barry's voice, sounding as if he was speaking through fuzzy cotton. 'Barry?' she asked.

'Sara!' he exclaimed in understandable surprise. 'Love, this is unexpected but rather sweet of you. I had an uneventful flight, nothing unusual.'

She had to laugh. 'That's not why I'm calling, you muttonhead!'

He grunted. 'Figured as much, but you can't blame a fellow for trying. What's wrong? Spent all your money already?'

'I wish it was that simple. Barry, I had a midnight intruder last night.'

A brief silence. 'Are you all right, babe? You weren't—I mean, nothing occurred—oh hell!'

'No, I wasn't raped, if that was what you meant. I couldn't sleep and when I heard someone in the living room, I crawled out my bedroom window and ran to a neighbour's house. We came back later and things were ripped up in my bedroom, but nothing was stolen, and frankly that scares the hell out of me. Barry, I'm afraid it might have been someone who knows who I really am.'

He asked her, 'Are you coming back right away? Where are you now, at a motel?'

'No, I'm back at the house getting a few things.'

'You little idiot!' he exploded. She had to hold the phone receiver away from her ear slightly. 'Of all the damn-fool things to do, that takes the icing right off the cake . . .'

'Hold your spittle, Barry,' she protested, chuckling. 'I've a very big and very black Dobermann panting at my side at the moment, and I don't plan on staying.

What I'm calling about is to tell you that I'm staying a while longer in the area with a friend, and if you want to get in touch with me just write here. I'll be over for mail every day. But Barry, use my real name, just in case someone decides to look at my mail. Also, I want you to do something else for me. Do you remember those crazy fan letters that I was getting around six months ago?'

'Sure, I remember,' he responded immediately. 'Do you think the guy who wrote those could be your intruder?'

'I don't know. He would have had to fly out here to do it, but if he happened to be following me, then I suppose anything is possible. What I want you to do is to find out for me. Hire a private detective from there to check out the fellow—I think he lives somewhere in Pasadena. The letters are filed with the rest of the fan mail. It's a good thing we've made a point to keep it all! Barry, I want whoever did this found out, and I don't really care how much it costs. Do you realise how my freedom could be impaired if we don't find out who did it? I would never know if I was safe or not!'

A sigh wafted over the receiver. 'I know, babe, I know. I'll get someone checking on that fellow right away. In the meantime, though, couldn't you get in touch with the local police and tell them who you really are? I think you need some protection, kiddo.'

She smiled. 'For the moment, Barry, I have protection. Don't you worry about me. I'm not going to go to the police unless something dire happens. That has to be avoided at all costs right now. Don't ask me to explain.' It would be, she thought, disastrous. 'My friend called the police this morning and they've already been here to dust for fingerprints. The place was clean, so there's no lead here. I'm afraid it's up to you.'

'And I'm half a continent away!' he groaned. He would be clutching at his hair, she guessed.

'Let go of your hair and relax,' she said calmly, and grinned at his startled exclamation. 'Private detectives know how to board planes, too, you know. If they happen to come out here, get a message to the house somehow and I'll try to arrange a meeting time with them. Tell them to stick it under the garage door—I've got the car and the garage is empty, so there's no reason for anyone to try to break in. We can work out something, I'm sure. I've got to go now, Barry. See you, and thanks, old boy.'

She had nearly replaced the receiver when she heard distant yelling. She brought the phone curiously back to her ear. 'Whoa, Sara! Don't you want to hear about contract negotiations with the television network? I think they're going to agree with your demands, kiddo. They're breathing fire and stomping around right now, but I think it's just a ritual rain dance, nothing more. Sooner or later we're going to have 'em!'

'That's great, Barry,' she said warmly, not feeling half as good as she might have at the information. 'I'll get in touch with you. 'Bye!'

She spent the rest of the time cleaning out her refrigerator, packing up all the perishable foods in the car to take back to Greg's. When she had everything in cartons in the back, she checked once more in her bedroom to see if she had left any clothing that was undamaged, and she found stuck in the back of the closet a dress and a pair of slacks that she threw over her arm. Then, whistling cheerfully at Beowulf, who fell pantingly in beside her, she opened the front door—and shrieked at the dark shadow of the man that was standing before her, blocking out the sun.

Strong hands gripped her as, in a panic, she tried to back up and run away. Beowulf snuffled a greeting at Greg's feet. He pulled her close for a quick minute, then let her go. 'I'm sorry,' he said softly, taking the clothes off her arm and slinging them over his. 'I didn't mean to scare you. You were a long time, and I got worried. Everything all taken care of?'

She put a hand over her pounding heart, taking a steadying breath. 'I think so. Just a minute. If I fall over in a faint, you know that I've had a cardiac arrest, nothing big. Just call an ambulance.'

He smiled ruefully. 'And that was after I said I was sorry! Are you ready to go?'

She wrinkled her nose at him, nodding. He ushered her out then, and locked the door behind him. It was a blustery day, with sudden, unpredictable gusts of wind that tore right through their coats and whipped their hair into tangles. Greg opened the passenger door for her without asking, and though she raised her eyebrows at this, she slid into the seat anyway. He then climbed in and started the car, backing swiftly.

They put the food away quickly. Sara had apples in her cheeks from the outside wind and her eyes were very bright. Greg kept looking at her, and she caught a few of his glances. Finally, laughing with embarrassment, she said, 'What's the matter, do I have birds nesting in my hair, or something?'

He gave a silent snort and she saw his chest heave. 'No. Do you want to go for a drive?'

Her eyes lit up at the suggestion. 'What a nice idea! Yes, I would, thank you.' He swatted her on the bottom.

'Then go and comb your hair and get your coat again, little girl.' It was her turn to snort, and he was laughing when she left the room.

Greg pulled open the door to the garage and let Sara sail on through, a few minutes later. She sank into the passenger seat of his car and ran an admiring hand across the leather upholstery. Then he was beside her, revving the engine slightly, and they were travelling down the lane and soon pulling out on a main highway. He increased the car's speed until they were travelling at a nice steady pace, then he leaned back as if to say,

'That's it. We're on our way,' and Sara put her head back on the headrest, relaxing.

She was soon in a very strange state, almost surrealistic. The ribbon of the road was coming towards her continually, and threading under the car to disappear behind her. She was oddly alone and yet not, at the same time. She felt free to think her most private and closely guarded thoughts as if she were by herself, but she had none of the sense of loneliness that usually accompanied such thoughts. From time to time she glanced sideways at the strange and strangely familiar man next to her and found him silent, concentrating on the road and yet seemingly relaxed as well. She felt him, felt his presence and awareness and peace of mind, almost as if she had telepathy and was inside his mind, thinking his thoughts, feeling his emotions.

It felt as if they were two separate manifestations of the same being. If was as if they coexisted only side by side, and she knew that he felt her presence as intensely as she felt his. She was aware of every glance he gave her as if he had reached out with his hand and touched her on the arm. She knew him intimately.

Presently she fell asleep.

Someone was lifting her, holding her, carrying her carefully. She stirred and, without opening her eyes, put her arms around the neck of the man she was so close to. 'Mmm, hi,' she whispered into his ear, and he rubbed his cheek against hers.

'Hi.' He deposited her on the couch in the den and genty removed her arms from his neck. 'Are you hungry?'

'No,' she murmured drowsily. 'I'm sleepy. What time is it? You know, I'm always asking you that.'

'It's rather late. I'm going to fix us a light supper and then I think you'd better go to bed.' Greg glanced at his watch and frowned at her. Circles shadowed her eyes. She looked washed out.

Trying to hide her yawn, she apologised, 'I'm sorry I

fell asleep—I just got so relaxed that I kind of drifted away. Boring, huh?'

Greg sat beside her and took one of her hands. It was easily engulfed by his larger one, and he played with the fingers absently. 'No, it wasn't boring. I was hoping the drive would relax you and it did. Mission accomplished. What would you like for supper?'

'I'd rather just go to bed.' Her eyelids were so heavy, she couldn't keep them open any longer and she shut them just for a little rest. He left her curled up on the couch as he went to the kitchen to prepare a light snack of soup and salad for them both.

Sara was in a light comfortable doze when a slight noise, a tiny shuffle, a noise barely acknowledged in her consciousness, had her heart pounding and her stomach flipping over in that terrible and familiar way. It was just like last night, and she bolted up from the couch with a cry of terror. Blundering into the hall, she grabbed at the wall for support, then Greg was crashing out of the kitchen to stare at her.

'What happened?' he snapped, looking around and appearing to her to be very dangerous suddenly. She didn't consider him as a personal threat any longer, however, and she rushed to him, crying.

'I don't know, I was almost asleep and then I heard something and it sounded like last night—I–I'm sorry, I couldn't help myself,' she babbled miserably, the easy tears of exhaustion slipping down her cheeks and splashing on her sweater.

His face gentled. 'Sara, calm down. You were probably dreaming, sweetheart. Look around you, there's no one here. See, Beowulf is calm. He doesn't miss anything, and he'd be the first to know. Sara, it's okay. You're safe, do you understand me? Safe.'

Her eyes clung to his face, needing to hear the words of reassurance and to see that look of unruffled calm. He talked to her for a few minutes more, soothingly

and easily. She suddenly giggled and saw his face
change. 'I'm so stupid!'

'No. Perhaps a little unsettled, but never stupid. Come
and keep me company in the kitchen—I have some soup
on to warm.' He perched her once again on the high stool
and gave her lettuce to cut up into two serving bowls. She
was soon finished with the job for her fingers were
graceful and quick. Greg saw her involuntary glance at
the black rectangle of glass that showed the dark autumn
evening outside and, moving casually to close the curtains
so that nothing showed, he started light chatter, soon
having her respond in a normal fashion. They ate in the
kitchen, as they had that afternoon. Greg poured her wine
and she sipped with appreciation.

'Mm—tastes like mine,' she told him.

'It is,' she was informed complacently. He chewed a
minute and swallowed, grinning at her mock outrage.
'We'll have mine tomorrow,' he soothed, reaching out
and refilling his own glass. Sara snorted.

'We'll have to, since this was my only bottle. You
know, I'm really beginning to wake up now. Greg, tell
me about yourself. I know virtually nothing about you.'
She was looking for his facial expression to change, to
shutter up, and was ready for it when it did. The open
look in his eyes was replaced with the wall. She said
quickly, 'Don't misunderstand me. I don't want to
know anything that you don't want to share with me,
really! I just want to know what you like to do, what
you work at for a living, what you like to eat, besides
omelettes, soup and salad, and if you're up on your tax
payments to the government, that's all.' She felt him
start to relax, and she let herself smile a little. 'I know
one thing about you already.'

'What's that?' His eyes were still shadowed.

She waved a fork that had lettuce speared on it. 'You
cook a mean omelette, buster, and chop an incredible
onion. Such style!'

He smiled involuntarily. 'I like to cook. I like to listen to music, especially classical and rock. Jazz is a relatively new experience to me that I'm learning to enjoy more and more. Country and Western music, I can do without.'

Sara gurgled, 'Amen to that!' She wondered momentarily at his odd twisted smile at that, when they raised their wine glasses for a solemn toast. It was forgotten easily, though, as a light tinkle shivered down her spine when the glasses clinked. 'What do you like to read?'

He lounged back against the counter behind him, balancing his wine glass precariously. She watched with fascination. 'Eastern poetry.'

Her eyebrows arched delicately. 'Oh, really?'

'Don't look that way, you unenlightened chit! It's good stuff, very philosophical. Of course, I like a good thriller now and then, too.'

His dark eyes sparkled at her evident amusement at that. His hair was tousled casually, lying on his collar in a mussed-up fashion, and his shirt gaped open several buttons down, showing a glimpse of the brown chest that she had seen so briefly last night. She twinkled wickedly at him, feeling a happiness course through her veins like wine. 'How very erudite of you! William Goldman, I'll bet.'

'Yes, and Ian Fleming's James Bond series. There's a collection in my study, if you're so inclined.' He nodded at her encouragingly.

Her expression was wry. 'No, thank you. I've had enough excitement to last me for a few weeks, I think. Tell me something else.'

'Unfair, unfair,' she was told mildly. 'You tell me something about yourself, or I'm a clam.'

She rubbed her eyes with a thumb and forefinger. 'Let me see. I'm a sucker for a man in a three-piece, navy blue pin-stripe suit. Your turn.'

Greg raised his eyes to the ceiling and rolled them

around, then wagged a finger at her. 'Not good enough, missy. Try again.'

She chuckled delightedly and reached for the wine bottle to top her glass off. 'You'll have to give me a moment. What exactly are you looking for? Do you want a deep, soul-wrenching confession? ... I thought so, you horror ... How's this, when I was nine years old, I stole my mother's car keys and had a wreck.'

He looked immensely fascinated. 'You've got to be kidding. No? Were you hurt?'

'I've got a scar on my elbow,' she told him blandly, and rolled up her sleeve to show him. It was on her left arm and curved around the bone. 'I stuck it through the side window when I hit the tree. Mother came running out of the house while I was backing up, and she was screeching like a diesel train, and her mouth was wide open. It impressed me so much I forgot to watch the rear view mirror and I ran over a fire hydrant and then into an oak tree. Bet you the tree is still bent, too.' She grinned as he roared with laughter. 'Of course,' she confessed with a trace of embarrassment, 'I probably would have run into the fire hydrant and the tree anyway, because I only knew how to work the car in reverse. I hadn't learned yet that there was such a thing as a gear shift involved ... Your turn.'

Greg had to take a minute to calm down. The bottle of wine was nearly gone and he poured the rest into their glasses equally while he pondered the subject deeply. 'I don't know. Don't throw that at me, I'm thinking! I'm thinking! Okay, here it is: in grade school I put putty in the front door locks of all the houses in my neighbourhood. Yes, seriously! I was grounded for a month, and had to write a letter of apology to everyone. My father wouldn't let me photocopy a form letter. It took me for ever.'

Sara concentrated on getting her breath back and

wiping up the wine that she had spluttered all over the table. Her face was flushed from coughing and laughing at the same time. 'And you were the favourite on the block, right?'

'Well, I had to learn to run pretty fast,' he admitted adroitly. He drained his glass and stood. 'Finished with that, yet? I'll take the glass. How about coffee and some cheese and crackers now?' At her affirmative, he pulled out the cheese from the refrigerator and the crackers from the cupboard. She watched while he sliced the cheese.

'I'm curious, Greg. How did they know who did it? Put the stuff in the locks, I mean. Were you caught in the middle of the act?' She spooned coffee into the maker and switched the button. Her nose wrinkled at the aromatic smell of new coffee making and fresh pungent cheese, and she perched on her chair with a cracker in her mouth.

His lips twisted wryly. 'No, I wasn't caught, I was too good for that. I opened my big mouth and confessed. I'd done it on a dare ... what did you think, that I cooked up the zany idea on my own? Here, open your mouth—like that cheese? I worried myself sick for about a week or so and finally broke down and blurted the whole story out, conscience-stricken villain that I was.'

Her eyes regarded him smilingly. 'And you felt better, I'll bet. 'Fess up, you did, didn't you?'

His mouth twitched in self-mockery. 'I felt worse, especially when my parents raided my piggy bank for money to pay for the locks that were ruined, but at least I started to keep my food down after meals and sleep nights.'

The coffee was done and soon poured. They both duly sipped and savoured the hot brew, swapping stories and looking into each other's eyes. The truth of the matter was that Sara never really tasted her coffee, and barely paid attention to the cheese and crackers she consumed. Her mind was focussed on the man opposite her, drinking in every one of his mannerisms. She watched his hands gesture out in emphatic thrusting movements when he got involved in a subject. She loved the understanding look in his eyes when she confessed her childhood isolation, and her loneliness when her mother died. She delighted in his laughter and she revelled in his sense of humour.

Finally, though, she was forced to call an end to their late-night conversation when she found herself yawning more than she was talking. Her eyelids drooped and her head felt fuzzy. She was so tired that she felt not the least embarrassment or selfconsciousness when Greg walked her up the stairs, his arm around her waist. It was what she had wanted anyway, and she leaned her head on his shoulder. She had stiffened up while they had sat talking, and her muscles ached badly. 'I suspect,' she groaned to him, 'that I might have broken something when I tripped and fell last night.' At his swift look of concern, laughter bubbled up and overflowed when she gurgled, 'Maybe we'd better go to the beach and see if I really did break something!'

He rubbed her cheek in a way that was becoming endearingly familiar to her. 'You're very, very tired, I think. I hadn't realised that you fell last night, although I should have guessed at the amount of bruises you had when I tucked you in bed . . . Sara?' She lifted her head with an effort to look at him. They were at her bedroom doorway, and he reached around the wall corner to turn the light on for her. 'Beowulf will sleep on the rug by your bed, and I'm just in the next room. If you feel you need to, leave your door open, and I'll leave mine open too. Call me if you're worried, hmm?'

She sighed, nodding, and with a swift kiss on her lips that was quite brotherly and yet at the same time left her tingling, he was gone. She barely went through the motions of brushing her teeth, and pulled on her nightgown carelessly, crawling between the sheets in record time. She had left the door open, and she fell asleep with her hand dropped down on Beowulf's silky head. She was not alone in the house. Just the knowledge that there was someone breathing, sleeping, caring nearby made a wealth of difference to her peace of mind. She felt secure.

The dog's whine had her rolling over to bury her head in a warm soft pillow. The masculine chuckle had her lifting her head and opening her eyes. The smell of coffee had her turning over and sitting up. The sight that met her sleep-blurred eyes had her giggling insanely.

Greg, wryly smiling, approached the bed with a balanced cup of coffee in one hand. He was very correct and quite handsome in his pin-striped navy blue suit, with a crisp white shirt on underneath. She took in at a glance the expensive cut that emphasized broad shoulders, graceful body movements and long muscular legs. His hair was brushed and still wet from a recent shower, and it lay sleekly against his well-shaped head, making his jawline seem more prominent. He concentrated on setting the cup and saucer down gently, then he too sat on the edge of her bed.

He told her, running an appreciative eye down her slim neck and shoulders, 'You look all ruffled, like a little bird caught the wrong way in a strong wind. Are you always this cheerful in the mornings?'

Sara tried to control her mirth. 'It's just that you're wearing a pin-striped suit,' she attempted an explanation. 'It struck me as funny somehow.'

He looked down at himself and appeared to start. 'Good heavens, so I am!' Then he chuckled deeply as she endeavoured to hit him with her pillow. He fended it off easily with an agile twist of the wrist. 'I have to go to town for a while today. Will you be all right on your own, or would you possibly like to come with me? If you'd like to come, you'll have to hurry, I'm afraid.'

She relaxed against the headboard of the bed. 'I thought you put the suit on as a joke,' she confessed with a grin, 'after what I said.'

'I did,' he told her. 'You don't think it was sheer coincidence, that of all my suits I would pick this one, do you?'

She had to giggle. 'I wasn't sure.'

He looked at his wrist watch, and the movement made her look at it too, but she found herself looking at the strong corded wrist instead. Dark hairs curled around the gold band. 'I'm going to have to leave soon. Did you want to come along?'

'Where were you going, Three Oaks?'

'No, I was going to travel farther south to Niles.'

Sara thought for a moment. 'I think I'll just stay here with Beowulf.' She dropped her hand over the side of the bed and patted the dog's head affectionately, and he thumped the floor in response. Greg looked at the two of them wryly.

'Why do I get the impression that I've lost my dog for ever?' He touched her face gently. 'I'm going to leave, then. Make yourself at home. I should be back in about three hours.'

He was gone, and silence settled over the house like a mantle. All Sara could hear was the sound of her own breathing, the tick of the bedside clock, and an occasional sigh from the dog on the floor. Sunlight flooded through her window. It was deceptively bright, tempting her to throw open the window and bask in the warmth, but she knew that if she were to open it, all she would get would be a chilly blast in the face, so she opted for a shower instead.

She thoughtfully soaped her back and shoulders as

she considered the affectionate side of Greg that she had recently seen so much of. Granted, she had been in need of some human understanding and support lately, but she was still a little taken aback at how Greg had responded so positively, with such affirmation. It was another apparent contradiction in the man. He definitely puzzled her. First of all he seemed to make a sweeping rejection of all strangers, and then he had accepted her—no, even more than that. He had actually invited her to come back to his land, and then into his house. An act of hospitality from an apparently hostile man. Then, too, his compassion and understanding friendship were at odds with the wall that she had sensed in him, the repelling of all observances, his self-imposed isolation. She sensed loyalty and integrity in the man, and an inborn instinct of caring for others. He was like a mathematical sum that didn't quite add up, no matter how she manipulated the numbers. He was a puzzle with missing jigsaw pieces. Why did he seem to accept her, of all people, a total stranger? She felt the need to find out.

She was too afraid to find out.

She dressed in a skirt with a low hem for a change, instinctively cloaking herself in her own femininity as she did every time she was unsure of herself. It was a deep red cotton skirt with a flounce at the bottom, and she wore a pretty white blouse with ruffles at the neck and wrists. Then she carefully applied eye make-up, enhancing her strong, arched brows and deepening the hollow under her brow-bone to make her eyes appear huge. Then with a quick glance around her room at the mild chaos, she soon had the bed tidied and her clothes put away. She dusted too, as an afterthought.

Deciding to skip breakfast, she went for a tour of the house, restless, anxious for something to keep her hands busy. Finding some cleaning materials in the downstairs closet, she looked wryly down at her red skirt, mentally shrugged her shoulders, and lightly dusted through the downstairs, whirling swiftly through the rooms. She straightened the den, washed the few dishes in the sink, and eventually found herself drawn to the closed door that opened to Greg's office.

She peeped in, as hesitant as she would have been if he were really there, and nearly turned around to leave again. It was as if she were violating the man himself by coming into his room like this, but she couldn't help herself. It was a comfortable room, with a big antique wooden desk and padded chair, and a dark brown motif carried throughout the furniture and carpeting. Two walls were lined with bookshelves that were filled with books. She smiled at the collection of Ian Flemings on one shelf, absently noting that they weren't in alphabetical order. She idly pulled one out to look at it, and put it back in the correct alphabetical order. Soon she was pulling out all the books and slipping them into order, and the shelf looked better to her eyes. It matched her sense of regulation and organisation.

Sara was a very neat person. She put her shoes in order, lined up pair by pair in the closet, and she never left her room out of place. She was the type of person that would reach out and straighten a painting in someone else's house if it were crooked. To some people, this characteristic would drive them crazy, but she could never understand this. She just liked to have things neat, and to put them where they belonged. She also liked to have something to work on. When her hands were busy, she could be content to think; It was her favourite form of relaxation.

Some time later she was earnestly working on the bottom shelf on one wall, her legs curled up beneath her and skirt tucked neatly in at the ends, when a noise made her look to the doorway. Greg was there, casually leaning against the doorframe with his jacket slung over one shoulder and his white shirt partially unbuttoned.

He watched her with a sardonic eyebrow cocked, mouth level.

'I suppose it would be a waste of time for me to ask you just what do you think you're doing?' he asked, his tone dry and unemotional.

She started guiltily, a book in each hand and dust on her nose. Her eyes were huge and startled, and she looked like a child about to receive a scolding. 'I'm—just straightening up a little,' she said, and looked down at her hands as if they were about to do something completely unpredictable. She missed the fleeting look of amusement that passed over his features in an uncontrolled quiver, and they were soon impassive and unreadable.

The books that had resided on the bottom shelf were stacked up around her and penning her into a tiny corral. She was peeping over a stack that just reached her chin level. Greg sauntered leisurely over and looked at the reorganisation of the other shelves without saying anything. Sara's face grew longer and longer, her mouth drooping ever so slightly, her eyelids sliding down to hide her expression.

'I'll never be able to find anything in here again,' he sighed mildly, and draped his suit coat over the back of one chair.

She felt miserable. It truly hadn't occurred to her that he might have enjoyed things the way they were. It wasn't in her nature to be content when she thought that something needed organising. 'I'm sorry,' she said in a low voice. 'I thought you'd like it.'

He was rolling up his shirt sleeves to the elbow, perusing the other bookshelf on the opposite wall. 'How much more do you have to do?'

Her head snapped around and her eyes widened. It looked as if he had every intention of digging in and helping her! 'Er ... I'm about done with this bookshelf.'

He pulled over a chair and stood on it. 'Then I'd better pull down these books from the top shelf, or the next thing I know, I'll be driving you to the hospital because you've broken your leg.' This time Sara caught the definite amusement in his voice, but she didn't take offence. She was too busy feeling relieved.

She started to smile a ridiculous, foolish, delighted smile, and mentally shook herself. Rearranging her features as best she could, she answered mildly, 'I'd appreciate it if you would.'

They spent the rest of the morning in this fashion. Sara gave a satisfied sigh as she took one more swipe at the bottom of the second book shelf, dusting the rearranged books in a busy manner. Greg was leaning against his desk, attentively. 'Feel better now?'

Bustling about had eased her feeling of selfconsciousness after he had entered and found her thus, and she grinned saucily up at him from a kneeling position, eyes sparkling and dark hair tousled. 'Much! Now it's time to start something else, though.'

But at that he was shaking his head emphatically. 'I don't know about you, lady, but I'm about ready to start gnawing at the woodwork, I'm so hungry! You do what you want, but I'm having lunch.'

Sara sat back and began to notice the emptiness in her midriff. 'You know, I'm rather famished myself. What is there to eat?'

'Let's find out, shall we?' A cursory inspection of the refrigerator revealed plenty of sandwich material, a leftover salad already prepared, and Greg produced several different cans of soup ready for her inspection and approval. 'Not exactly haute cuisine, I'm afraid.'

She raised an eyebrow, picked up a chicken soup can from his hands, and deftly whizzed it through the can-opener. 'So what? I happen to like chicken noodle soup from a can. Not very well bred of me, I suppose, but I also happen to like hot dogs and hamburgers.'

'. . . and making sand castles, wading barefoot on the beach in October, sleeping with a pillow hugged to your stomach——' he murmured, laughing.

Her face went red at this last statement, and she stammered, 'How did you know that?' He calmly took the open can from her unresisting fingers and pulled out a saucepan from below the oven.

'I woke you up this morning, remember?' he taunted gently, dark eyes snapping merrily at her expression. 'And I've looked in on you before—just to make sure that you were all right, of course.'

Her face changed and she said sarcastically, 'Of course! How remiss of me to forget. I——'

'And,' he went on smoothly, appearing to concentrate on the amount of water he added to the pan, 'a very sweet sight it was, too. You all curled up in the middle of the bed, hair all mussed up and cheeks all flushed and a little tiny smile just hovering around the corners of your cherry red li——'

She saw his own lips twitching then, at her even redder complexion, and said hastily, 'Yes, well, all right, that's enough of that. What are you going to do with the rest of your day?'

His face straightened immediately into sobriety, but she detected a devil lurking in the depths of his eyes. It made her wary. She wasn't sure how to treat this new side of Greg's personality. She didn't know what to expect.

'I have some work to do in the basement,' he told her innocently enough. 'I carried a lot of firewood downstairs yesterday. That ought to take care of my afternoon, more or less, together with taking out the tree stumps from the two trees I felled. What do you think you'll do?'

She was setting the kitchen table with two soup

bowls, plates, and cutlery, arranging things precisely. Greg noted the neatness with a swift uncontrolled grin. 'I don't know,' she answered indecisively, sighing. 'I'm not very used to having time on my hands like this.' Her eyes travelled restlessly around the kitchen. 'Is there any housework that needs to be done?'

'Well,' he considered her question with an overtly serious face. 'I have some clothes that need washing, if you have any you'd like to do, too. And, if all else fails, you can always reorganise my kitchen cupboards.'

Her eyes rested thoughtfully on the closed rectangles of wood drawer. 'That's an idea. Maybe I'll do that.'

'Why don't you?' His voice sounded slightly strangled, and she looked up at him sharply.

He coughed a little. 'Are you all right?' she asked, and he nodded. The soup was ready and he poured it with an unsteady hand. She said, 'Maybe you're coming down with a cold?'

His eyes twinkled at her. 'I think I am.'

After lunch, Greg hurried up the stairs to change, and Sara rummaged around the place for an apron to put over her skirt. Failing to find one, she took a towel and tucked it in her waistband. Then she looked over his cupboards with an assessing eye. Her senses felt violated at the way his heavy pans were stacked carelessly in the bottom cupboards, and she was shoulder-deep inside, rummaging around, when he re-entered the kitchen on the way to the basement. He saw a neatly curved bottom and an enticingly slim waist protruding from below the counter, and couldn't resist the impulse that came over him.

Sara started up so violently that she hit her head on the top of the cupboard shelf. The slap on her rear had been sharp and totally unexpected. She backed out of the cubicle and rounded on Greg, her cheeks flushed and her hair awry. 'Why did you do that?' she demanded snappily.

He took her hands and yanked her up to a standing position, catching her against his chest when she swayed momentarily, caught off balance. 'You have a very cute bottom, madam,' he told her, nose to nose, 'and it was sticking out all by itself. What self-respecting male could resist such an invitation?'

'It wasn't an invitation and you know it!' was her only retort, as she looked into deep brown eyes and found herself quite distracted. She had calmed down amazingly. 'And besides, you're pretty darned lucky I didn't take off your head by slapping it so hard it wouldn't land until it hit the Mississippi river!' Her words were getting softer and softer in spite of the biting content, because his lips were approaching nearer and nearer. Her eyes fluttered closed and she put her face up for the kiss. It came, and then another and another flitted by as he brushed her lips gently, teasingly, as light as a butterfly alighting. It was delicious, tantalising, and unsatisfying. Sara's eyes flew open as she felt his lips withdraw and his arms loosen. Then she squealed in outrage when a playful heavy hand descended on her bottom again.

'Get back to work, woman!' Greg growled softly, mock-threateningly, laughing at the expression in her indignant hazel eyes. He looked so incredibly good laughing that she had to blink.

He was at the door before she could react, however, and she muttered disgustedly, 'Hell, I'm beginning to feel married!' She was looking at him, but her words weren't meant to be heard and were spoken quietly to herself.

His hearing must have been very, very sharp, because he did hear what she said, and he turned slowly to look at her, one heavy eyebrow cocked. The look in his eyes, the frankly sexual appraisal, made her go warm all over, and a slow, burning tingle suffused her from head to foot. 'Oh, no, you aren't,' he told her softly. 'Not by a long shot, you aren't.'

He was gone, and she was staring at the empty doorway without seeing it for a long time afterwards.

# CHAPTER SIX

THE afternoon fled quickly for Sara, busy as she was with arranging the kitchen to her idea of orderly neatness. She stood back finally, though, a gleam of satisfaction in her eyes, and surveyed the inside of the cupboards, now meticulously arranged. It was not that Greg was unclean by any means, she had found. It was just that now there was a method to the grouping of spices on the top shelf, and the glasses were within easy reach instead of being so hard to get at.

She took a glance at the clock in the stove and began to fix coffee. Greg had been outside for some time now, working on the tree stumps, and after sticking her head out to call to him a question and feeling the nippy air, Sara thought a cup of the warm brew would do him good. She carried it to him when it was made, and he cupped it gratefully with both hands.

'Ahh!' was his only comment after taking a drink, but it was a very satisfied sound. Then he said, 'That was just what I needed, sweetheart. How's the reorganisation of the kitchen coming?'

'Just fine,' she told him, 'I've got everything done now. You should see the spice shelf! Everything is in——'

'Let me guess, alphabetical order, right?' he interrupted, grinning. His hair was tousled and his breathing a bit laboured from the strain of chopping at a deep exposed root. His chest rose and fell deeply, and she could see a fine film of dust on the part that was exposed to the air. There were bits of dirt stuck to the side of his corded neck, and she absently took off her apron when she saw it, wiping his neck with the corner of the towel. He submitted meekly to her ministrations.

117

'You're going to get a chill in this cold wind if you stop for very long,' she told him, grimacing at the soil on the towel and shivering a little herself. 'How long will it be before you're inside?'

Greg surveyed the stubborn tree root thoughtfully. 'Another half an hour should see it out. I want to lay down some sod from the forest, though, and that will take me a little while longer.'

She looked curiously around. 'I thought that you said there were two tree stumps you wanted to take out?'

Greg turned her around and pointed over her shoulder to an area about twenty feet away. 'See the disturbed ground over there? If you go and look, there's a bit of grass that's about seven feet in diameter that I just laid down over the filled-in hole. That's how I want this patch to look when I'm done with it. That way, in the summer there won't be any scars in the area, only an extension of the grass, without having to plant seeds.'

Light dawned. 'Oh, I see. You know, I've lived most of my life in the city, and I'd never heard of that before. It's ingenious!'

He finished his drink and handed her the mug back. 'Thank you. You'd better run inside before you get chilled.' With that, he bent and picked up his axe again, shaking his head to get the hair out of his face. Sara laughed at him and reached over to smooth it back out of his eyes, running her fingers through the unruly front lock.

'There you go. What do you want for supper? I'll fix it.'

He surveyed her doubtfully. 'Can you cook?' He sounded as if he wondered if she could even pick up a pan, and she shook a finger under his nose in retaliation.

'Now you've gone and done it!' she warned. 'You've made me mad. You'll be lucky if you get a boiled egg—just see!'

He was instant humble contrition. 'I was only teasing a little, honest. Please don't feed me a boiled egg, Sara. I don't like 'em.'

She considered his humble stance loftily. 'We'll just have to wait and see. I don't know whether I'm still mad at you or not. I'll decide later.'

She was totally unprepared for his swoop down on her, and she shrieked with delight as he scooped her up in his arms and twirled her around and around. 'You'll decide now, madam,' was his grim warning, 'or you won't set foot in that kitchen again without my supervision and intervention!'

'Oh, yes,' she cried, clapping her hands like a child. 'Let's have Supervision and Intervention instead of boiled eggs! I won't boil you an egg for supper—Greg, stop twirling me around, I'm getting sick! You goon, I'll throw up all over your shoulder, I swear it!'

He stopped suddenly and the whirling world soon settled into proper perspective for her, but not before she watched it go round a few times without her. She kicked her legs experimentally, but Greg refused to put her down. He looked deep into her eyes. They were so close their cheeks nearly touched. 'You really aren't mad any more?' he asked, sounding disappointed.

She backed her head up to look at him better, puzzled. 'I was never mad to begin with and you know it! What are you getting at?'

He shrugged and the movement sent her bouncing up once, making her remember how she was being held. She wriggled again, thinking it must be a strain on his back to hold her so long off the ground, but he only tightened his grip on her shoulder and under her knees, making it clear that he had no intention of letting her go for the moment. 'It's just that if you were truly angry with me, we could have kissed and made up,' he whispered, bringing his lips closer and closer. She shut her eyes as his dark head descended and met his lips eagerly with her own.

Greg slowly let go of his grip under her knees, and she slowly slid into an upright position, his other arm tightening on her shoulders and pulling her hard against his chest. His free hand came to her hair and entangled itself at the back of her head, forcing her to deepen the kiss. She made no protest. Her arms were around his neck, her two hands at his nape. She felt his shoulders hunch, drawing her to his lean body, and she was aware of being set down gently, but her feet were barely touching the ground and Greg was supporting her whole weight against his chest. His legs were wide apart for balance, and she was flat hard against every part of his long, powerful body.

The kiss changed, became pulsing and urgent for both of them. They explored each other's mouths with an excitement and tenderness and a total mutual consent.

For Sara, it was the first time that she had ever been completely concentrating on, and vibrantly aware of, another human being. She was lost in the embrace, drowning in sensation, overwhelmed with physical desire and emotional communication. She couldn't explain it to herself; certainly she wasn't able to at that time, and she couldn't later examine her feelings with any degree of coherency. All she knew was that she wanted to be near this man, wanted to be close to him in his thoughts and feelings. She wanted to reach out her hand and feel his close over it. She wanted to make love to him and give the greatest gift she could possibly bestow on him—herself. She felt no fear at their closeness, nor of her own overwhelming feelings. She knew instinctively that Greg would never hurt her, and she felt, so close as she was to him now, that he was experiencing some powerful emotion himself. She felt it course through him like an electrical charge, making him shudder against her slim body, making him crush her against him with arms like bands of steel. It was a mutual experience, and it was right.

Slowly, very slowly, she was lowered to the ground until she could feel the earth beneath her feet, and she was held gently, very gently, until she could stand on her own. Her head was leaning on his shoulder, in the warm shelter of the curve of his neck. She snuggled her face deeper into the strong column, putting her lips to the pulse pounding there, caressing it lightly. The hand in her hair tightened behind her head, pushing her harder against his neck as Greg heaved a great sigh. She tasted the salt of his sweat, then he was pulling her away from his warmth with a wry twisted smile. Held a little distance away from his encircling arms and the warmth of his chest, Sara felt suddenly very cold. A slight wind touched her and she shivered. She was watching his face, and she saw the rather blind look in his eyes gradually fade away until he was grinning down at her, back in control, noting her chills.

'You'd better run inside, madam, before you catch your death out here,' she was told prosaically. 'And let me get back to work with no more distractions!'

She tossed her head, sending her black hair tumbling in a glorious gleaming swirl, greenish colour glinting in her eyes. Greg suddenly saw the temptress in her, the quality of sensuality that the press was able to catch in her sultry poses, the aura that the camera picked up with such sensitivity. He stood as if stunned, staring at her, unable to tear his gaze away. Sara backed away from him a few steps, hair still tumbling, caught in the wind and blown across her face. Through a cloudy curtain of darkness, he saw the mocking slant to her eyes and got the impression of curved lips. She pushed the hair off her forehead.

'So that's all I am to you,' was her murmured reply, 'a distraction? Something to be used and experienced and then forgotten when one is working on other ... more important matters? Hah!' She was laughing inside at the expression on his face, the total concentration

and fascination in his eyes. She knew that she was more
than a mere distraction to him and that his choice of
words had been teasing. Some irresistible imp had got
hold of her, though, and she intended to tease him back
for such an implication. She raised a saucy, wagging
finger to him. 'Honey, if you think this is distracting,
you ain't seen nothin' yet!'

She didn't need to turn around and look back as she
re-entered the house, walking slowly, almost insolently.
She knew and could feel his eyes burning on her back
all the way into the house.

She wasted no time when she reached the kitchen, but
immediately set about preparing supper, deciding on a
casserole of gratinée potatoes with chunks of salty ham
liberally added in. After putting the dish into the hot
oven, she made up a quick batch of homemade biscuits
to go on the bottom rack in the oven. Then, while the
bread baked, she deftly cut up a lettuce salad, adding
bacon bits, onion, and tomatoes to it, and slipped it
back into the refrigerator. Then she considered the
dining room table. They had eaten in the kitchen
before, on the everyday plates, but she wanted things to
be a little more special than that. She rummaged
around in a polished oaken cabinet in the dining room
and came up with a lovely set of bone china. It would
look beautiful. The table was quickly set and the
biscuits rescued from the oven's intense heat, a
temptingly golden crunchy brown. Sara covered them
with a clean cloth and glanced at the clock. She wanted
to be absent from the kitchen when Greg came in. She
had a surprise for him. She didn't have much time, so
she hurriedly washed some fresh fruit and cut it up for
dessert, adding the package of walnuts she had found in
the cupboard when she was organising everything.
Then, before she dashed upstairs, she peeped in at the
casserole. It was cooking nicely and would be fine for
some time.

She then looked out of the window to see how Greg was progressing, and found him gathering up his tools. Sticking out her head, she yelled to him, 'Dinner's in about an hour. That enough time for you?'

His head lifted and turned. 'It should be fine!' he called back. 'I'm just finishing now, and I'm going to take Beowulf for a quick run, before cleaning up!'

Sara nodded and pulled back in. The fruit salad was put into the refrigerator and the counters cleaned and wiped off, then she was galloping up the stairs. There was just enough time. In her room and closing the door, she contemplated the open door of the closet with a secret smile. With a quick decision so characteristic of her, she yanked out an outfit and laid it across the bed. A silky pair of gossamer-thin pantyhose floated after it, settling softly on her pillow. Then she had drawn out a black pair of shoes, and clean underwear. Heading for the bathroom, she took a quick shower, thankful that she had washed her hair that morning. A few pins held it securely on her head while she swiftly cleaned up.

Then she was sitting in front of the large dressing-table mirror, contemplating her clean face. Greg had never seen her with more than just a minimum of make-up on. In fact, he had never seen her dressed up at all. With a return of her old caution, she knew that she didn't want to wear her make-up as heavy as she did when she was performing professionally. It wasn't her personal preference anyway. She reached for a jar of foundation and smoothed just enough on to even out her complexion a bit. It didn't take much, for she already had a smooth silken quality to her fine clear skin. The foundation added just a bit more creaminess, making her appear alabaster white and very fragile against the thick dominant blackness of her curtain of hair. Then she touched her cheekbones with a blusher that, when blended skilfully and subtly, gave her the appearance of a fragile porcelain doll.

She used a brown eye-shadow that gave her eyes depth and softness, and lined her eyes with a smoky black liner that she then smudged delicately. Her eyebrows were strongly marked and yet refined, so she left them alone. A few applications of black mascara made her lashes so long that they touched her cheeks when she looked down. She lined her lips, then filled in with a red rose colour that matched the shade of her blusher, then sat back to stare at her reflection critically. It would do; it would definitely do. Then she contemplated her hair, hanging like a straight waterfall. It would go up tonight. Her fingers moved swiftly and soon her hair was lying in a heavy complicated coil on her slender neck, emphasising the graceful curve of her nape and the slight curve of her cheek.

The outfit she slipped on was black, a deceptively simple black skirt that foamed into a rather wide fall around the mid-calf, and fitted tightly at her slim waist. The blouse was filmy and transparent, needing the delicate black chemise underneath for decency, and it complemented both the skirt and her white skin perfectly. It was long-sleeved, allowing the white glimpses of her arms and upper chest to gleam through the gauzy black. Lastly the shoes were slipped on. They were a black leather pump style, with low heels and a small silver bow on top. She continued the silver motif with a slim silver belt that clipped in front, and silver chunky earrings at her ears.

Greg knocked on her door quickly, and she called out, 'Yes?'

'I was just checking to see where you were,' the deep voice reverberated through the wood. 'Supper smells delicious!'

'Thank you. I hope it is delicious. I need to go and see about it,' Sara returned, stepping back and looking at herself. A slender vision of delicate beauty looked back, eyes huge, expression doubtful. How would Greg see her? Would he like what he saw?

'I'll be right down. I want to clean up and change,' he told her, voice fading away. She heard his bedroom door slam, and decided to go right down so that he wouldn't see her until he was downstairs.

She slipped ice into water glasses and set a chilled bottle of wine in a bucket of ice on the buffet cabinet by the table. Then she put out the biscuits and served up the lettuce salad in side bowls. She had just carried in the bubbling, steaming casserole dish and had set it carefully on the hot pad ready for it, when a noise from the doorway had her turning gracefully. The skirt flared slightly as she moved.

Greg was at the doorway in a position that indicated he had been there for some time. He had changed into a dark pair of well-fitting slacks and a white shirt with a cream pullover sweater over it, and his hair was still damp from the shower he had just taken. The sleekly brushed hair that lay so close to his well-formed bone structure emphasised the rugged, slightly irregular quality of his facial features. She found herself fascinated by his firm, unsmiling mouth. He exuded masculinity, and she was as sensitive to the fact as if she had been a receptive radar.

He looked brooding, intent. His eyes travelled over her as if he couldn't see enough. She simply stood still, waiting for his perusal to end, waiting for some kind of reaction. He came away from the door with a slow, sensuous grace, his eyes never leaving her face. When he stopped, he was very near, his head bent to her. She could have leaned slightly forward and been fully against his chest, but she didn't. She just stood as if she were stone, only her living eyes moving, watching him.

'You're beautiful,' Greg said huskily, deeply. That was all, a simple straightforward statement. Sara was used to fulsome flattery, extravagant utterances from all types of people, and she didn't credit any of those kind of remarks with the truth, but Greg's elementary statement sounded as if it had come right from the heart, and it pierced her to the quick. She reacted instinctively, immediately, by putting one hand against the side of his face. His own covered it. A smile grew in his eyes and he told her, 'It's a good thing I looked in here before I went upstairs to change for dinner. I was able to get the idea from the table setting that I should dress. You, of course, weren't going to say a word.'

She laughed up at him and shook her head. 'I was getting back for that remark you made about being "just a distraction" and I was going to hit you for all I was worth! A total surprise was the only way.'

'It worked,' he said, smiling. 'You've floored me. Go ahead, walk all over my poor devastated body!'

'Don't be silly. As long as you've got my point, the matter is finished,' she replied flippantly, and sat down in the chair he held for her. Deep down, though, she knew that it wasn't finished. Something had started outside, in that chilly October wind. Things had just begun.

Greg was flatteringly appreciative of the meal, and he made huge inroads in the casserole dish before him. She watched with a smile. Her own appetite seemed to have diminished, and she contented herself with a small helping and a few bites of salad. She nursed her glass of wine, for the most part just content to keep him company.

They talked, and found that they had a great deal in common. They both loved outdoor sports, and were conscious of their own body's fitness and health. Both seemed to like the same kind of movies. Both expressed an interest in their environment, and a deep concern for the gluttony and wastefulness of the general public. Sara found that she could converse well with Greg, and she didn't hesitate to state her thoughts and feelings with a frankness and an intelligence that earned her a gleam of respect and admiration from him.

She in turn was astounded at the depth of perception and keen understanding of the human mind that Greg possessed. His thought processes, she found, were clear and well organised, with a neatness of precision and a definite logical pattern to them. He was extremely well educated and informed on many issues of the day, and he tended to be hotly argumentative on the subject of politics. He would never let her make a careless or thoughtless remark without some kind of proof or explanation to back it up. He was quick to respond to her remarks, even getting to the point of anticipating some of them as he became familiar with the way her mind worked. He became uncanny at this, until she protested finally that he must be a mind-reader, to anticipate her reactions so well.

His reply to this was amused. 'No, I'm not telepathic. I can just sense the direction of your thoughts when you're thinking logically and unemotionally. Anyone can do it when a certain knowledge of a person's likes and dislikes, interests and prejudices, is acquired. I'm beginning to have that kind of working knowledge of you, and so I can anticipate your reactions to certain subjects at times. You've got to realise, though, that when you're dealing in the realm of human emotion, reactions and responses are infinitely varied and unpredictable. I could no more predict you than I could a total stranger. Oh, I don't mean straightforward subjects. I'm fairly sure that if you were confronted with the sight of an animal being physically abused in public, you'd raise all hell, but the reason I know that is because I've seen the kind of gentleness and considera- tion that you treat Beowulf with. Therefore, I know that you harbour some love for animals in general, for dogs in particular. The kind of unpredictability I'm speaking of is the type of emotion that springs from associations with one's past, dealings with relationships, and things of that sort. No one tells another person every single thing about himself or herself—it's impossible. Thus, to some extent, we are all strangers to one another.'

The wall, she thought, resting her chin on her laced fingers and staring off into nothing. It's that damned wall every time. Even now, when he's being open, intelligent, and as honest as he can be, that wall rears its ugly head. He'll retreat behind it whenever he's tired of me, or whenever he's hurt.

I have the same kind of wall, though, don't I? Sara asked herself candidly. Haven't I been hiding behind my image for six years, being, with the few friends that I have, the Sara Bertelli in private that I am in public? And aren't I even right now playing out a certain role, hiding from Greg who I really am, afraid that he won't understand that other part of me? That's what it is: I'm afraid that Sara Bertelli will scare away the chance of a real relationship. She's blocked so many before. She's isolated the plain and simple Sara Carmichael in me until that part of me nearly died away. But they're both a part of me, both the public and the private. They both express in different ways who I am inside. The one can't die without the other. And Greg is only seeing a part of me now, but at least he's seeing the truth. He just isn't seeing the whole.

'I don't agree with you,' she said quietly. He had been watching intently the expressions that had flitted across her face, and hadn't been able to interpret them. 'I don't believe we're all strangers from each other. For the most part, yes, I'd have to say that I've closed off my personality from much of the world, letting them see the package on the outside,' and she gestured down at herself, 'but not the person on the inside, and I think you have too. But I also believe that there comes a time when one can say, "Yes, I will be totally honest and completely open with this person, because I want this person to accept me for what I am, all the faults and feelings, all the quirks and qualities that make up what I am." It's hard, though, and some people never really make it. The reason why is that they don't open up completely, and so they aren't giving themselves totally to the relationship. I can understand that. Total honesty leaves one totally vulnerable. It leaves one open to rejection, because there are no guarantees. The other person can back away for whatever reason is considered valid, and it would leave a scar so open and raw in the one that it could virtually cripple the emotions for life. It's frightening, isn't it? But, you see, the little unpredictable starts in a person, and the mistakes, and the inconsistencies that you're talking about, they don't really matter in the long run, if the core of the person is known and loved.'

Her voice was melodious in the suddenly silent room. She felt Greg's silence and utter stillness from where she was. She felt his tenseness, and his complete concentration on what she was saying. She felt the urgency, and the inexplicability of it struck her, but she didn't question him. She merely finished what she had to say and calmly stood up to clear away the plates for dessert. How Greg took her words was up to him. She had communicated herself as best she could.

In the kitchen, she stacked the dishes in the sink and went about the motions of starting coffee. The silence in the other room was beginning to bother her. She wished he would say something, anything. She wished he would open up, tell her about himself—not the mundane everyday occurrences and events, but tell her why he was so closed off. She wanted ... she didn't want to think about what she really wanted.

The coffeemaker was burbling and she started to dish up the fruit salad. A noise from the doorway had her turning, turning very slowly, because she wasn't sure she wanted to see what was there. Greg stood immobile in the doorway, and he looked at her briefly, rigidly.

There was a light jacket clenched in his hands. Sara had just enough time to register shock, then he was saying, 'I need to take a walk. Hold my coffee for me.'

That was all, as simple and unadorned as his other statements. He was gone, out of the back door and into the darkness, before she had time to react. She sat down slowly on one of the stools by the butcher block table. It was, she suspected, going to be a long evening.

Beowulf came and leaned against her knee, whining softly, his large eyes anxious. Sara smiled at this and patted him on the head. She worked from the front to the back area behind his ears, scratching in the places he especially liked, easing his troubled doggy mind. He sighed, sniffed a bit at the floor by her feet, and settled down for a snooze. She watched him for a long time, noting the restless nose, the twitching tail. He whined once or twice, picturing, no doubt, some running rabbit, some past glorious chase. How simple life was for him! she mused. Life, for him, was to be enjoyed in a mad, dashabout way. He would gallop through his early years, trot happily through his middle years, and walk sedately at the last of his life, by his master's side. Greg was steady, gentle and firm with the dog. Beowulf had no worries beyond the enticing smells carried on an afternoon's breeze. How marvellously simple and carefree!

All the same, she was very grateful not to be living that kind of life. She wanted all the pleasure and the pain that her own life would give her. She felt a brief spurt of compassionate affection for the dog's simple mind, and then forgot it. It slipped away as easily as the summer days slipped into autumn, leaving behind perhaps a gentler and more understanding view for the animal's confinements and liberties, for his unswerving loyalty to his master.

She poured herself a cup of coffee and, finding herself in need of serenity and some sort of comfort, went into the den and put on some music. She picked classical and then looked through Greg's other albums, curious to see if he had any of her own. He had several; in fact, he had the greater part of her work, and she felt touched by this somehow. It seemed that without even knowing it, he was attracted to that other part of her personality. She curled up on the couch and tucked the ends of her dress neatly around her. Beowulf settled on the floor, having followed her closely into the next room.

After a while she put some logs on the fire and was soon staring deeply into the flames that were constantly shifting and changing. The fluid movement of the yellowish-red fire was mesmerising, hypnotic. It freed her mind from troubling thoughts and left her relaxed and mellow.

When Greg came quietly into the room to sit beside her, she didn't even start.

As if they had never stopped having an easy conversation, she asked him idly, 'What do you do for a living, Greg?'

Silence for a while. She felt him relax as the warmth of the flames seeped insidiously into his chilled limbs. A quick glance showed that his hair was ruffled and blown about his rugged face. A reflective mood seemed to have settled over him, and he looked to be more at peace with whatever had been bothering him. She reached out a hand and his strong cold fingers closed over it.

'I was a criminal lawyer for several years,' he said quietly, leaning back against the couch and closing his eyes. 'I also inherited some money, and have been retired from the actual court practice. I've written two books, one on the American criminal justice system, and the other on the political structure hampering the justice system.'

'It sounds utterly fascinating, and a little frightening,'

was her response. She looked at him, realising how much of his personality was wrapped up in the lawyer part of his life. It affected his whole thought processes. His mind was so clear and sharp and quick. She shuddered to think of his formidable intelligence used as a weapon. 'Did you defend or prosecute?'

'Both, eventually. My last case was defence.' His replies were brief, but not necessarily dampening. He was just being as simple and as straightforward as he had always been, getting quite devastatingly to the heart of the matter.

'Do you think you'll ever get back to it?'

'No.' He turned his head as it lay on the back of the couch and looked at her. His dark brown eyes caught the glow of the fire, and it made them brighter than usual, like twin dark flames. Sara could see into the depths of the colour, and it wasn't as dark as she had thought, but instead a honey shade, warm, compelling. 'Sara, I——'

She spoke at the same time. 'Greg, there's something you must know——' They both stopped and just looked at each other. Her heart began to thud in slow pounding strokes. His fingers were lightly stroking her wrist; he must feel her heart race, feel how fast her pulse was going now.

Then he was saying huskily, 'No. No, we'll talk later. But now, Sara, I've got to kiss you, I've just got to, I——' He shook his head impatiently, hauled her over to him in an abrupt manner, wrapped his arms around her tightly and brought his mouth down on hers.

An emotion swept over her so strongly that she was carried away by its tide. She didn't even struggle. This was what had been started, she thought hazily, this is what I wanted all along. Something came to her then, and she struggled both to sit up and to clear her mind enough to be coherent. 'Greg, I've got something to tell you,' she began, but was effectively cut off by another deep, long, mind-weakening kiss.

'Not now, Sara,' his voice came to her, spoken low against her temple, roughly, urgently. He was pleading with her for something and she didn't know what. With every caress, every movement to pull her bodily closer, he was telling her an immensely important message without words. He needed her. He needed her now, tonight. Tomorrow faded away like morning mist. He wanted her physically, yes, she could feel that, but emotionally he needed her.

It was all out of control when it had started. She had lost all desire to withdraw before he had even re-entered the house. All she had been doing was waiting for him to come back to her, and he had come, just as she had known he would. Whatever devil he had gone to exorcise had vanished for the moment, the wall left completely behind. His mouth was inside her blouse, searching, caressing, kissing, and she was lying back on the couch with his hard weight on top of her. He raised his head, looked into her eyes, and she knew she was seeing to the core of the man. It was a naked look, more so than any naked body could appear. She knew him in that moment and then knew herself. This was no infatuation.

She loved him.

Greg carried her upstairs, her head falling against his shoulder, her hair draping them both like black satin. There was no hesitation in his steps; he didn't have to ask. He had asked her with his eyes down on the couch, and she had already given her answer, as wordlessly as he. He paused at his closed door, expression lost in the darkness, and quietly reached out a hand. He carried her in and put her very gently down on the large bed that was his. She had never been in his room, had never seen what it looked like, and she now waited in the strange darkness with an odd trembling in her limbs and a weakness pervading her mind and body.

She couldn't tell him the truth. She opened her

mouth to tell him and she couldn't. He undressed her carefully, with many caresses and soft tantalising kisses. Then he undressed himself, standing by the bed to shed his clothes, and Sara remembered the odd feeling from long ago, from only a few days ago, when she had seen him as being a monolith in the night. It came back to her when she saw the faint gleam of his powerful body in the near total darkness. He was strength.

.It was a night of giving.

He was so gentle with her, as if he knew, and at the same time so urgent. There was warmth and tenderness and emotional sharing. There was intense, earth-shattering, wrenching passion.

He stopped when he found she was a virgin. His whole body froze into a shocked stillness, and he began to say very quietly, 'Oh, my God, oh my dear, sweet God—Sara!' Then he was loving her, and the world dissolved into the rhythm of his loving. Afterwards, she thought she could feel a single drop of wetness slide down her neck, where he was resting his head.

They fell asleep

Greg woke her in the middle of the night; she didn't know what time it was. She opened her eyes to darkness and the safe, delicious feeling of being held very close. Her head was on his warm hard shoulder and his arms were wrapped tightly around her. His hand was cupping her head.

'Sara.' The whisper barely reached her, and she sensed it rather than heard it. She felt the movement of his chest come out like a sigh, when he whispered her name, and she opened her eyes. Her hand came up without her even realising her own impulse, and she was delicately tracing his face in the dark, like a blind person. Her fingers came to his lips, and he kissed each one.

'I wish I'd been a virgin too. I wish I'd known that you were. Did I hurt you?' The question sounded anxious, and she had to smile.

'Only a little physically and not at all emotionally,' she told him gently. 'And you were a virgin in a way. It was the first time you'd ever made love to me.'

That made him groan deep in his throat. Sara had to laugh aloud at that, huskily, and his bare arms squeezed her until she coughed a protest. He let her go for a moment, then rose above her and began to kiss her neck. She responded immediately by running her hands over his long torso in a sweeping caress. He said just one more thing. 'Dear heaven, how you got to be twenty-eight years old and still be a virgin with this body, I'll never ever know . . .'

She pulled back. 'I never really wanted to before.' Of course, after that, she didn't have a chance to say anything for a long time.

Sara woke up first in the morning.

The curtains were pulled together, but a sliver of light still managed to slice through, and it streaked blindingly across her eyelids. She moaned and rolled over and really woke up with a shock when she came against a large warm, hard body as naked as her own. Her eyes flew open and she surveyed Greg's sleeping form with tenderness flooding through her at the thought of the night before. Her body ached strangely, and she could no longer ignore the urge to move in an effort to relieve some cramped muscles. Carefully sliding out of bed and standing with a painful yet luxurious movement, she stood staring down at him. He was on his back, with his head turned to one side, and her heart lurched as she looked at the glossy brown hair she had stroked, the strong, graceful curve of the neck, his broad brown shoulders and the fuzz of hair on his chest. He was wonderful to look at. She let him sleep.

After a quick shower in her own room, she dressed and, driven by some restless urge, clicked her fingers to an eager Beowulf after leaving Greg a note. She needed to clear some things up in her mind.

She sat restlessly at the piano in her cabin, later, and played a few bars of one of her favourite songs. Why was she feeling such agony and regret this morning? Why was she wrenched with feelings she didn't want to acknowledge?

She was beginning to understand not just the morality of the decision to wait to have sex until after marriage, but also the emotional reasons. She had just made love to the man she loved. She loved him more than anything, it seemed. But there had been no word of love from him. There had been many tender murmurs and the memory was good, but there had not been one word of love. It must be nice, she thought sadly, to know that every morning when you got up you would see the one you love in the bed beside you. That assurance, that long-term faithfulness—she craved it. It could make for a whole lifetime full of the kind of loving from last night, manifested in different ways and not all of them physical. Now, the morning after, all she felt was loneliness. She was so unsure of him. It was the saddest feeling in the world.

She came to a decision then, and made several calls. The first was to Barry, and Sara listened to his news patiently, with some relief. The man who had written her the crazy fan letters some time back had broken down and confessed to breaking into her house, and he was being dealt with. Also, the contract had been argued out, and all it needed was her signature. She promised him, 'I'll probably be there by this evening, Barry. See you.' Her next call was for a plane reservation.

Some time later, after a long refreshing walk on the beach, she walked into Greg's house, from the back door. He was there, smiling a quick greeting to her as he stood by the counter, sipping coffee. She wished she could smile back at him as she nodded in response to his offer of coffee.

He handed it to her, and she cradled it in her hands for warmth, covertly studying his relaxed face. She said to him, her heart thumping strangely, 'A slight problem has come up in my work, Greg, and I need to make an overnight trip back home to take care of it. Do you think you could possibly drive me to the airport this afternoon?'

In spite of a cowardly impulse making her want to stare into the murky black depths of her coffee, something impelled her to watch his face for a change of expression. It came. His face slowly grew rigid, tense, the jaw muscles bunching spasmodically once before his expression turned to stone. His body had sprung into rigidity too, coming upright from the counter. He nodded once, briefly, swallowed his coffee, and walked with measured steps to the door of the hallway, and it was his very lack of outward response that bothered her so deeply.

The wall had snapped up into place again.

# CHAPTER SEVEN

GREG didn't protest; Sara wished he had, instead of looking at her so emotionlessly. He didn't utter a word about it, and she eventually went up to her room to pack an overnight bag with a leaden heart. She wasn't exactly sure what had happened inside him, but she knew that if she were to walk out the door right now with all her possessions, he wouldn't lift a finger in objection. It hurt.

She quickly had everything she needed in a small bag with shoulder straps, and she carried it down to deposit it on the floor in the hall. Unhappiness ate at her insides, but she determinedly wore a casual, normal expression. It was hard, but she managed it.

Lunch was unspeakable. She could barely force the food down past her resisting throat in the face of Greg's unrelenting silence and rigidity. When she mentioned the time of the afternoon flight, all he did was nod absently, his eyes shadowed, looking as if he were far away.

When he went into the hall to put her luggage into the car, he stopped suddenly, and she collided into his back. He turned, gripped her arm, and apologised, but his head was still facing her one overnight bag, and his apology lacked emphasis. Then he asked her sharply, 'Is that all you're taking?'

Her eyebrows shot up, and she felt puzzlement when she looked into his face. 'Of course—it'd be stupid to take anything more. I'm only going to be gone overnight, and I'm staying at my apartment.'

He closed his eyes and, incredibly, a look of relief passed over his features. Then he started to shake his head slowly and chuckle. 'What a total, stupid, idiotic fool I am!' Then he was holding her and kissing her hard, just like she had wanted all morning. He rubbed his cheek against hers and it was smooth and fragrant. She liked his aftershave. 'Sara, you'll have to forgive me for acting like an idiot this morning.'

'Okay,' she said simply, and gave him a sweet smile. She was still acting casually, but in truth, his sudden approachable behaviour was making her want to sing from pure happiness and relief.

He leaned his forehead on hers. 'I got the bright idea that you were leaving this morning and not coming back,' he confessed softly, rubbing his thumb along the base of her throat. Sara started to laugh at that and he grinned wryly, self-mockingly.

'But you're driving me to the airport and I'm leaving my car here!' she exclaimed in protest against such illogical and erroneous thinking.

'I know, I know. It didn't sink in at the time, but only when I saw your luggage and realised that you were leaving most of your clothes here did I realise how stupidly I'd been thinking.' He had bent and was exploring her neck with his mouth as he spoke, and she closed her eyes.

'You're right, you are a stupid fool,' she sighed. 'Mmm! We have to leave if I'm going to make my flight.'

He murmured reluctantly, 'I suppose so. Are you sure you have to go? Couldn't you ... stay for an afternoon nap?' She leaned against him fully, and his legs parted to take her weight.

'I'd like to, but I can't. I promised them I'd be there by tonight,' she whispered, and he slowly straightened up. It wasn't necessarily true. She could have had Barry send the contract to her by registered mail for her signature, even though he preferred her to sign in his presence. But she was feeling the need to get away from Greg's drugging influence. She needed to take time to be by herself, to think things out. And, she thought, it would probably do him a world of good to have time alone too. At the moment, though, all she could feel was regret for having ever made the plane reservation. All she could think of was the shadowed room upstairs and the things she had learned from Greg last night.

But he was pulling away from her, with one last kiss, saying resignedly, 'If you have to go, you have to, I guess, and I'm not making things easier for you.' No, she thought, you've complicated my life infinitely from the moment I first met you, Greg Pierson. You've messed up all the order, and the peace, and you've driven away my isolation, so why do I feel so terrible? What happened, between the magic of last night, to the shadows of the day? It was at the moment unanswerable, and she sighed.

Her depression seemed to manifest itself physically, and she felt draggy, worn down. She wanted to sleep.

They delayed until finally there was no more time to waste, and she had to board the plane. She turned to Greg and opened her mouth to say goodbye, but the words were never uttered. He took her shoulders roughly in a way that somehow spoke of desperation, and hauled her hard against him for a quick, instense, starving kiss. Then he was letting her go and backing away. For a moment all she could do was just stand and stare at him walking away, shaken, scared for some reason, and so totally alone she could have died from it.

She turned too and quietly boarded the plane.

Southern California was a climate shock to her senses. She called a taxi and gave him her home address, settling back in her seat to blink bemusedly at the blinding sunlight and the glaring traffic noises. This was what she had missed for the first few nights in Michigan! It was incredible. She had dressed wisely, putting on a light dress underneath an autumn coat, and she had shrugged that off some time ago. The Los Angeles traffic was crazy, the air dense with smog, the freeways winding and intersecting. She felt as if she had been through a major war by the time she had let herself into her spacious apartment. It was empty.

It was a shock as she looked around the light, tastefully decorated penthouse apartment. She had never even given a thought for its emptiness before. It had been a haven then, a place to run to when everything got hectic. She could shut the door and be alone. Now it really struck her just how alone she really was. Greg was two thousand miles away.

It was early evening, but she was so tired out, she crawled into bed and fell right asleep.

Sara shot up and grabbed for the ringing phone, knowing immediately who it must be. No one else was aware that she was back, unless he had blabbed it out to someone. 'Hello, Barry,' she sighed.

'Hey, are you all right?' he asked, instead of greeting her. 'You sound as if you have a cold.'

'It's no cold. I was taking a nap. The flight wore me out,' she replied, glancing at her luminous clock. 'All flights flatten me, you know that. Sorry I didn't call to let you know I was here—it slipped my mind.' She felt lethargic, heavy, as if she had a fever, and her mouth tasted like lead. She shouldn't have gone to sleep. She hated it when she slept too heavily and woke feeling this way.

'Don't worry your little mind about it, love,' she was told calmly. 'Have you had supper yet? Elise is fixing a great meal, and we thought you could come over for it. It'd give us a good chance to talk about things.'

'All right,' she agreed listlessly. Her head was aching.

'You sure you're all right?'

'Don't coddle me, Barry,' she told him irritably. 'You know I hate to be fussed over.'

'Well, okay. See you around seven-thirty? 'Bye.'

Sara weaved her way to the bathroom and stared at her reflection with disgust. Her face was flushed and her eyes too bright. A reluctant hand to her forehead told her that she definitely had a fever, and she cursed fluently. She took out a thermometer and found it wasn't as bad as she had first thought. She only registered a hundred-degree fever and, having done it many times in the past, she popped a couple of aspirin in her mouth, grimacing at the bitter chalky taste. She never stopped unless she was literally dropping in her tracks, and she had worked ten and twelve-hour days with temperatures such as this.

Not really caring how she looked, Sara dressed casually for dinner; the only trouble she went to was to take the time to coil her hair into a knot. She did take the effort to hide the blue shadows under her eyes, but the make-up went on like cake and she rubbed it off again. Her skin looked papery white, and felt dry to the touch.

Elise answered the doorbell and stood surveying her thoughtfully after inviting her in. She was a thin, small woman, with reddish hair, high cheekbones, and snapping brown eyes. She tended to wear heavy make-up. 'You look terrible,' she told Sara brusquely.

She didn't bother to deny this. She sank on to the cream couch gingerly, feeling the throb of pain at her temples. 'I feel worse than I look,' she said dryly, accepting a glass of wine. 'If you can imagine that.'

Elise excused herself so that she could go and check on supper, and Barry ran a critical, assessing look over Sara's half-reclining body. 'It's a good thing that the network's officials didn't get a look at you like this. They'd have ran so fast in the other direction, we wouldn't have seen them for dust!'

'Thank you, my loyal agent and manager, for those kind and understanding words of wisdom,' she muttered, then had to laugh. She had just told him that afternoon that she couldn't stand to be coddled, and he had just taken his cue from her. 'Where's that contract that you're panting to have me sign?'

Barry's eyes lit up and he went to go and get the paper. They spent the rest of the time before dinner discussing the different terms of the contract, and Sara had to admit that it was very satisfactory. All her own specifications had been met, and the fee ended up being very enticing. Barry spoke of the negotiations with his own satisfaction evident in his voice. He had the right, she granted; he'd done a good job.

Still, she found herself very reluctant to sign the paper. Barry had gone into the dining room to help Elise with the final preparations, and she sat alone on the couch, looking at the rectangle of white before her. Once she signed, she would have an obligation to fulfil. Did she really want that, after all?

She could have sworn she had effectively put Greg out of her mind, but unbidden, it seemed, his dark visage swam before her. She didn't really understand it. All of her being longed to be back on that quiet and lonely shore two thousand miles away, walking hand in hand with a big silent man, a loner, with a stalking dog at her feet. All she wanted to have was the reassurance of his presence, for now and for the rest of her life.

But she wanted this. She couldn't give up this life. She wanted to go out on that stage and perform in front of millions of people, with dynamic music, pouring everything she had into it. She wanted to know that people could hear her songs, to know that she was able to communicate to someone in this way. She wanted to make music and, like any true artist, she wanted to be appreciated for that.

Sara slowly picked up the ballpoint pen that Barry had laid down, and signed her name on the dotted line. She was committed.

If either Barry or Elise noticed that she was unusually quiet during supper, they didn't say anything. She saw Elise's quick sharp eyes on the untouched food on her plate, and noticed that the other woman was being especially kind to her. Probably Elise just thought it was because she was feeling poorly. Sara wished she could believe that herself. Barry drove her home, and she appreciated his concern. She knew he thought she wasn't acting normally, but what was normal, after all? Her feelings and affections had undergone such a dramatic change in the past several days that she wasn't sure if she was in touch with herself at all, or if a total stranger had taken control of her body.

She fingered her baby grand piano in the darkness, back at her apartment. She loved Greg; there was no doubt about that. But the essence of her personality was in her music; she prayed he would understand that. She fervently hoped that things could be worked out, and yet she felt such a dread, a premonition. Looking out over the bright garish lights of downtown Los Angeles, she saw balmy sunshine on a deserted beach.

She felt like she was being torn in two.

Shivers racked her body, and she crept into bed like a lost child alone in a tossing sea.

She overslept in the morning, and when she looked at her bedside clock, shock rippled through her. Her plane flight was in an hour and a half. Sara made to jump out of bed, and she fell back sweating and weak on soaked sheets. The room danced crazily around in front of her blurred eyes, and this seemed so funny to her that she giggled a little before catching herself up sharply. This wasn't a time for hysterical humour.

With some effort, she managed to get to the bathroom and use the facilities, but it left her weak and shaking, feeling as if she had just run a marathon race. She groped for the thermometer very carefully, but ended up knocking several things on to the floor anyway. She was beginning to get alarmed; she couldn't remember the last time she'd felt so sick.

Bad news confronted her at the sight of the mercury reading, and she groaned softly. Her fever was sky-high, accounting for the weakness and distortion of space. Her fingers on her cheek felt papery dry, and her cheeks were burning up.

Sara thought of Greg, and his reaction when he had thought she was leaving and not coming back. Her thought processes weren't working very well at the moment, and the only thing she could think of was getting back to him, and being held in his strong and gentle arms.

He was safety. He was home. She didn't think of anything else but this. She didn't care about the future and she couldn't think of the conflicts that had troubled her last night. They had faded away with the night's darkness, and her brow furrowed with the effort to recall her reasons for her own anxieties.

It didn't matter; there was no time. She took four aspirins and swallowed them without a second thought. That should help her get through the next couple of hours; it had seemed to bring down her fever last night. Then she dressed in faded jeans and a plain blouse, pulling her glossy hair back into a ruthlessly tight ponytail. Her face no longer swam in the mirror, and she hoped this was a good sign. She did no more than glance at herself, though, and it wasn't a pretty sight. The area around her eyes felt tight and drawn, and there was a slight yellowish tinge to her usually healthy-looking skin. The blue shadows underneath her eyes now looked like bruises, and her lips were cracked and dry.

She stuffed a few things carelessly into her overnight bag and swept up her handbag. A quick call to the cab agency she used frequently ensured her a ride to the airport, and after a very short wait, she was climbing into the back of a battered car. The cabby was cheerful and talkative, and Sara fought the urge to scream at him to shut up, all the way. The trip was around half an hour long.

Her shirt was sticking to her back when she finally got out of the cab. The heat was intense, unseasonally so, and it hit her already overheated body in overwhelming waves. The pulse at her wrists and throat pounded painfully. With great concentration, she weaved her way through the bustling crowds. It seemed to take forever, but she was finally boarded and sinking into her spacious first class seat.

She dozed fitfully for the whole flight, refusing all food and sipping listlessly at the proffered drinks. As she stared with lacklustre eyes out of her window at the sunny, cheerful landscape, it suddenly occurred to her that she hadn't really eaten for a good twenty-four hours. Her last meal had been with Greg, yesterday, at lunch, and she had been so tied up in emotional knots that she hadn't been able to eat very much. She hadn't eaten anything last night. It seemed odd to her that she wasn't even hungry after such a time, then the thought just slid away. She was wrapped in cotton wool, and the rest of the world didn't matter any more.

Someone shook her gently by the shoulder and she opened huge dull eyes to stare at the kind concerned face of the young stewardess who had attended her on the flight. 'We're about to land, miss,' she was told firmly. 'You've got to fasten your safety belt.'

Her fingers fumbled to do so, and the young woman suddenly sat down in the empty seat beside her. 'You don't look very well,' she said suddenly, touching Sara's forehead with a tentative finger. 'You're burning up! Are you going to be all right?'

Sara smiled briefly, wanly. 'I will be, sooner or later. I had to get home, and couldn't afford to miss the flight, but I've got someone meeting me at the airport.'

The other woman hesitated. 'Well, it's good that you're going to be met, but I think I'll stay close by, just in case. Frankly, you don't even look like you could stand up! I think I'll just keep you company until your friend arrives.'

'Please don't feel you have to,' Sara attempted to demur, but much to her secret relief, the young attendant insisted.

The descent of the plane had her head spinning around and around, and it never really stopped spinning, even after all the motion had ceased and she was standing along with the other passengers in preparation for disembarkment. The nice young stewardess had to take care of several things, but when Sara carefully walked to the exit of the plane, she found the girl right along beside her. She really was very nice, Sara concluded fuzzily. She was obviously concerned and caring, and she made it known in the most tactful way. Sara could feel her watching and assessing her, and she knew that the other girl was wondering if she would have the strength to disembark, but she never so much as touched her arm. The stewardess stayed close by, though, and kept up an undemanding chatter.

The grey tiles on the floor kept moving in the oddest way, but with the knowledge that it was all her imagination and that the floor wasn't really moving at all, Sara was able to present the appearance of normality as she walked with the stewardess through the airport. It was much smaller than the international one in Los Angeles, and less crowded, but Sara was much weaker and just about at the end of her strength.

She had never really taken to travelling, and was never at her best on trips, and this second flight in as many days, on top of her high fever, had sapped all her energy. She felt her heart pound and her ears ring and she thought with a lurch, I'm going to faint, for the first time in my life. The walls receded in the most peculiar way, and she concentrated fiercely on staying conscious. It worked for a few moments. She was unaware of having stopped moving and that she was standing right in the middle of a busy wide hallway full of moving people. All she could think of was how ridiculously inappropriate it would be if she were to make like wet spaghetti all over the floor in front of so many people.

A voice called her name, 'Sara! Sara, what is it?' and she saw Greg coming to her, a frown on his face. She blinked huge tired eyes, and they filled with tears as she looked at him. His face blurred away. He was angry, but really she couldn't help being ill. She was trying her very best not to be.

The voices of the stewardess and Greg passed her by, and she knew they were talking to her, but she couldn't hear what they were saying, because that rushing sound was roaring in her ears again and the walls were sliding back—really, that was very bizarre! She couldn't remember any other building that did that. She felt so very awful that she took in a funny little breath and tried to tell Greg, 'I feel quite ill,' but all she heard was a far-off whimper as the darkness came in on a high tide. It all just slipped away.

All she wanted was to be held and to be loved, and she hurt so badly, all over her body. It made large tears slip from her closed eyelids, she felt so lonely and sick. Someone murmured, and she was picked up gently and carried into a building. At that, some of her senses seemed to become abnormally sharp, and she recognised every stick of furniture that they passed as Greg carried her into his house. It was all very strange. She stared foggily about, realised what must have happened at the airport, and she suddenly felt very frustrated and angry at the whole world. She hated being ill, like every healthy individual does, and she was a terrible patient.

'Put me down, dammit, I can walk,' she muttered

weakly, irately, and felt Greg's chest heave as he laughed under his breath.

'Ah, don't tell me you're one of those kind of invalids. I can see I'm in for quite a time,' he sighed deeply, and Sara felt an upsurgence of resentment. *He* was in for quite a time! *She* was the one who was ill!

He laid her down carefully, but she still couldn't quite control her wince. For some odd reason she felt as if someone had taken a sledgehammer to every part of her body, and then taken a truck to run over what was left. A quick blurry glance showed that he had put her in his bed, and she felt careful hands at her blouse buttons. He disappeared, and came back to draw a nightgown over her head. Her body burned with aching heat, and yet she started to shiver with a bone-clattering chill. With teeth chattering so that she could hardly talk, she tried to tell him just how badly she needed a drink, but she couldn't seem to get her words out right. Greg apparently understood, though, for he brought her a steaming cup of tea almost immediately. When that didn't warm her up, her brought her a few filled hot water bottles and tucked them in at her feet. She lay curled up as tightly as she could, shivering and shaking and nearly crying, she was so cold. Her joints hurt so that she needed to move them restlessly to provide relief, yet she could barely stand to uncurl. Greg frowned down at her miserable attitude, then pulled back the covers. At that, she cried out in protest, but she soon saw that he meant to get into bed with her. He drew her near and tucked her icy hands into his open shirt to get them next to his warm skin. She sighed from pleasure at that. Eventually, his body warmth and the hot water bottles thawed her out enough so that her muscles could relax, and she fell asleep, held tightly in his arms, his cheek hard against her hot forehead.

She opened her eyes much later to find herself alone. She hurt, just ached all over, and her skin felt like a furnace. She was so hot, just intensely burning up, that she threw off the covers with a moan and tried to stand. The cool air hitting her skin felt so good that she went to the window and fumbled to unfasten it, intending to throw it wide open.

A noise sounded behind her and a deep exasperated voice seemed to boom out in the confines of the room. 'My God, I leave you for barely ten minutes and you're trying to kill yourself!' She could hardly stand the loud noise, and covered her ears with a whimper. 'Do you want to catch pneumonia, Sara? Come on, get back in bed and cover up. Please!'

She turned and faced Greg, with her eyes very bright from unshed tears and her cheeks flushed red from fever. Her hair felt like an iron weight on her neck. 'You don't have to scream at me like that!' she whispered fiercely, clutching at the sides of her aching head as it pounded with the effort of speaking emphatically. 'And I'm not going to get back in bed, I'm going to get dressed!'

Greg eyed her warily, and with some amusement. 'You know better than that, Sara. You have a temperature of a hundred and four, and you aren't going anywhere except back in that bed if I have to tie you down to keep you there!'

The room was distorted slightly, seeming much bigger than she remembered. It looked like quite a long trip to get anywhere, and she felt like sinking down right where she was. It was too much effort to try for anything else. Greg seemed distorted too. He was bigger, somehow menacing, and he loomed over her, frighteningly close. Sara made a pushing movement with her hands, a futile gesture, and whimpered, 'Don't—don't come any closer! Please, I don't have any money with me . . . oh, God, please . . .' Strong arms caught her as she wavered and started to fall, and she shrank away fearfully from the support. Where was Greg? He had promised her she would be safe, and here was the intruder again. He was going to kill her!

She fought weakly, tears streaming down her face, and two hands held her carefully. Why was he being careful with her? Was he going to try and take her somewhere else before killing her? She couldn't seem to understand.

And then, strangely enough, her father was there. He didn't really look like she remembered him, but she knew it was he because he treated her with the same tender care that he always had in the past when she had been ill. He held her in his arms and coaxed her into taking soup little by little. She didn't want it, and she told him so, but he insisted, and she had always done what her daddy wanted her to. She asked him forlornly why he had to go away when she was only five years old. Didn't he know that she needed him? At that, he held her close, hugging her to him as if he would never let go, but eventually he did, and stood to leave her. Sara cried bitter, weak tears when he went away. He wasn't ever coming back. She knew he wasn't. She was afraid, and she wanted to get her mother's car and go to look for her daddy like she had before, because she just knew he was out there somewhere. But the effort to raise her head was too much, so she closed her eyes with the promise of trying later.

Someone else was there suddenly, and she started when cool hands touched her forehead with an impersonal kindness. A dark man lounged against the doorpost, his dark face intent and his eyes on her. The man touching her, examining her, pulled back the covers to see her body for some strange reason, and she shivered from cold at their removal. It didn't last long, and he was soon tucking her back up again, but all her hoarded body heat was gone now, and she shook from severe chills. Two warm bundles were tucked in with her presently and she huddled to their warmth. The two masculine voices that were, as before, abnormally loud. She wished they would go away. It hurt her ears to listen to them.

'Well, doctor? What do you think? I started to worry when I realised she was delirious, and thought you should have a look.'

A strange voice answered, 'She's pretty sick, of course, but I don't really think hospital is necessary just yet. It's that bad virus that's going around. It's a pretty typical case: extremely high fever, aching joints, some delirium, dehydration. Try to get her to take these, and keep forcing as much liquid as you can down her. The danger is, of course, if the fever doesn't break, in which case you can always call me. Also, like I said, dehydration. She's burning up all the liquid in her body. The cases that I've seen in the hospital have been the ones suffering from dehydration. I don't think she'll get to be that bad, though.'

'Thank you for coming, Doctor,' said Greg, shaking hands with him. 'I know you don't usually make house calls.'

'Well, I owed you one for the legal advice you gave me some time back, so I'd say we're about even. Give me a call if you need anything, or if she seems to worsen.'

At the end of her patience with the booming conversation going on right over her head, Sara snapped petulantly, 'I wish you'd stop yelling right by my ears! Don't you know that I'm a very sick person?' She covered her aching head with a pillow to shut out the mild chuckles that seemed to tear through her eardrums.

Barry woke her gently, and she rolled over to stare fuzzily at him. 'What the hell are you doing here, Barry? How did you know where I was, anyway?'

'Never mind that, sweetheart,' he said patiently, not sounding like himself at all. 'Here, I want you to take this pill for me—it'll make you feel better. I have something for you to drink, too.'

She rubbed her eyes; she felt so odd. 'I don't want it, Barry. I don't want to take drugs, dammit! I can make it without that kind of boost, Greg said so. Go away!'

He sighed, a sound that was torn between affection and amusement. 'Sweetheart, this isn't just a drug, it's medicine. It will help you get well again. Please, Sara, take it for me.'

She just looked at him owlishly, sombrely, set her jaw and shook her head. He pleaded with her, argued with her, but to no avail. She absolutely refused to take the pill. Finally she told him furiously, 'If you don't get out of my bedroom, Barry, you're fired for good, and I mean it! Oh,' and she suddenly crumpled into a little girl again, 'why don't you leave me alone? I'm sleepy, Daddy, and I don't want it.'

'Pumpkin, you've got to take it. I know you don't like your medicine, but Daddy has to go to work, and he can't sit around all day arguing with you about it.'

'I'm not a pumpkin,' she protested like she always did, and he answered in the same old way.

'No, you're a princess, aren't you? A princess in disguise, and someday the whole world is going to know how special you really are. But for right now, you're just a sick little girl, and you have to take your pill.'

'Will you stay longer, Daddy, if I take it? You won't go away, will you?' She was having the hardest time focussing her eyes. His face kept blurring and becoming somebody else's.

'I'll stay, sweet—I'll stay.' And he did, slipping into the bed with her after she had taken the pill and drunk the water. He settled back and drew her into his arms, and she snuggled as close as she could get.

'Momma died,' she whispered, and his cheek came down on top of her head. 'She never stopped missing you, Daddy.'

'I know, love. She's happy now, though. Forget it for now. Go to sleep now, Sara.' She did just that, content to be held. She wasn't alone any more. He would take care of her. Just who *he* was became confused in her mind and the father ghost faded away into darkness.

She dozed, woke up occasionally to peer un-interestedly around her, and dozed again. Someone was always there, giving her pills to take and liquids to drink, and he was someone different each time and yet the same person deep down inside. He took her temperature, and wiped her forehead with a cool cloth. He held her hand when she cried from the aching in her limbs, and stroked her restless hot hands until she slept again. It seemed to go on this way for ever.

Then it started to rain inside, and that was the oddest thing of all, because Sara had never seen it rain in a house before. She lay very still and let the wetness soak into her heated body, sighing as it cooled her and soothed away the burning. She fell into the first deep sleep she'd had in what seemed like a thousand years.

Greg came in and found her drenched with sweat. Her hair was limp and damp and her nightgown was literally soaked. The sheets were wet also, and he went about the motions of changing both the bed and her. He had to wake her up to get her nightgown off, and at this she protested volubly, but she was soon deep asleep in comparative comfort, curled up into a ball and tucked under clean sheets. Greg breathed a sigh of relief at the breaking of her fever, and dropped his clothes by the bed tiredly, crawling in beside her and drawing her close to his side.

She murmured once and rolled over to tuck her chin under his and reach for his hand. They slept.

# CHAPTER EIGHT

SARA awoke slowly, stretching luxuriously. It felt incredibly good to stretch without that terrible aching in her joints, as if she were rotting away from the inside out. She turned her head lazily and surveyed Greg's room with interest. It was tastefully furnished, with rich, dark wood coloured in the furniture, and light blue carpeting. Come to think of it, she thought, everything in Greg's house was plush and of the first quality. She liked that. It was nice how her taste and his seemed to coincide so often.

Greg came through the doorway right then, his eyes smiling down at her when he saw the sanity in her clear eyes. 'Hello, madam. Are you feeling any better today?'

'Lord, much,' she said calmly, sending him a sweet smile in return. 'I have this horrible feeling, though, that when I try to stand up I'll be as weak as a kitten.'

'You were a very sick little girl,' he told her, sitting down on the bed and offering her a glass of juice. She saw that it was orange juice, and she couldn't stand orange juice, so she put it on the bedside table.

'I seem to recall very strange dreams,' she mused, rubbing at her eyes with the heel of her hands. 'Did— do I remember a doctor coming here, or was that an hallucination?'

'No, that was reality. You were very rude,' he told her sternly, picking up the juice and handing it to her. She put it down again. 'You told us to shut up.'

She laughed. 'I remember now. You were practically shouting right in my ear, and the sound literally reverberated through my poor aching head. Was that the fever, or were you insanely yelling back and forth for the sadistic pleasure of seeing my pain?'

'It was the fever. You seemed sensitive to light too, and I had to keep the curtains closed so you wouldn't cry all over my pillows ... Sara, will you drink this juice?' That last was said impatiently as he tried to thrust the glass into her hand, but she refused it with a shudder.

'No amount of torture will get me to drink that juice, so you might as well take it back downstairs,' she informed him firmly. 'I was sick on orange juice as a child, and I can't abide the stuff. Do you have anything else? I'm parched as dry as a desert, starving too. Got any steaks?'

Greg drained off the juice with a shrug. 'You get soup and toast for right now, until your stomach has had a chance to get used to food again. You haven't eaten for at least three days.'

She ogled him. 'Three days! You've got to be joking! No? I was sick for three days? Lord, what a shock ... I'd just assumed that it had been about twenty-four hours or so ... I've misplaced three whole days!'

He retorted whimsically, 'Seems like three years to me. I've never had the misfortune to encounter a patient as terrible as you before.'

Sara was feeling a little weak, so she slid down the pillow gingerly, and gurgled, 'So sorry about that. I've always been just horrible when I was sick. I remember my father very well; he was the only one when I was very young who could get me to take my medicine. My mom used to get just furious at the way I would meekly take my medicine from him after only a little bit of coaxing when she would spend hours trying to get me to swallow the stuff.'

Greg was looking at her with an oddly tender expression, as if he was reliving some memory of his own, and she stared at him in puzzlement. 'When did your father die, Sara?'

She shrugged. 'Oh, I think I was around six years old.

He did a lot of travelling in his kind of work, and was gone a lot. One day my mother got a call long-distance. He'd been on a trip across in Europe and the airline was calling her to let her know that the plane had disappeared in the Atlantic. It was never found—I remember very clearly. They searched for a long time, and my mother flew to the East Coast. I stayed with my grandparents and played with their dogs.'

She shook herself out of the unhappy reminiscence and glared at Greg aggressively. 'I want a two-pound steak, medium rare, with five baked potatoes and three heads of lettuce cut in a salad. After that, I want five gallons of wine, assorted carbonated beverages, milk, water, and anything else you might have, except orange juice—yeuck! Then for dessert, I want twenty-five glazed doughnuts, with chocolate sprinkles on top . . .' She giggled as a finger flipped her nose.

'Soup, toast, and hot tea coming right up,' Greg said firmly, and disappeared. She was left alone to stare at the ceiling throughtfully. Beowulf came into the room and approached her hesitantly, and she watched him with some interest. He looked as if he were committing a major crime by slinking stealthily up to the side of the bed. Sara clicked her fingers at him, and was rewarded with a hearty lick from his long wet tongue.

'Ugh, you beast! What's the matter, boy?' she asked, scratching at his ear gently. 'You look like you're about to be beaten to death!'

'He should be,' said Greg, as he came back into the bedroom with a tray loaded down with enticingly aromatic somethings. She shifted in bed eagerly as he approached, and fell to with a will. 'I told him to stay out of this room while you were sick, because I was afraid that in your delirium he might scare you half to death. But I suppose it's all right now since you're in your right mind, more or less.'

She protested at that, around a mouthful of toast. 'I

resent that statement, counsellor. It holds unsavoury implications, and I just may have to sue you for libel . . .'

'In which case, madam, we shouldn't be holding a private discussion before the court date. I need to consult my attorney, and you should do the same . . .'

'Oh, baloney!' she snapped elegantly, and glanced at her tray with some surprise. The toast was nearly all gone, but she couldn't finish her soup if her life depended on it, and the tea was nearly untouched. 'I seem to have filled up rather quickly after all, Greg. I don't think I can manage any more—I'm sorry.'

He touched her cheek. 'Don't worry about it, sweetheart. It's understandable. Your stomach has shrunk. I'd have been surprised if you'd been able to handle much more. I'll just get rid of this tray while you settle down for a nice long nap.'

He whisked away the tray as she argued, 'Greg, I'm not sleepy. I want to get up and do something. My hair needs washing and I feel so sticky all over, it——'

'No,' she was told firmly, and her eyes took on a mulish expression at the autocratic tone. 'You're too weak, and it's too soon to get your head wet after the fever. It broke only a few hours ago. Just try to relax, will you? I'll be downstairs in my study if you need anything. Just holler, I'll hear you.' He kissed her forehead before leaving, ignoring her resentful expression.

She thought for some time after he had gone. She had resented his ordering tone of voice very much. Nobody ordered her around! She had come to the place in life where she gave the orders, and if she wanted to take a shower, then she would take a shower. It was a free world, after all, and her choice. With that firmly and aggressively worked out in her mind, she pulled back the covers and carefully slid her legs over the side of the bed. She couldn't resist the impulse to look over her shoulder, and that made her very angry. Why should she be worried at what Greg thought? He didn't own her.

Her housecoat was draped over a nearby chair, and she picked it up as she made her way slowly to the bathroom. Funny, how really weak she was, and how the distance to the bathroom seemed suddenly much more than she had first thought. By the time she had made it to the bathroom, she was sweating from the effort, and trembling with exhaustion, but she felt sticky and unclean, and she had it fixed in her mind that she was going to take a shower no matter what. Then she eyed the tub doubtfully. Maybe a bath would be better. And, just in case Greg was very angry, she would lock the door.

That accomplished, she leaned over the side of the tub and turned the water taps on full blast. The roaring, gushing, splashing sound of the water rushing to fill the tub had her jumping in consternation. That sound must be clearly audible throughout the empty house. Greg couldn't help but hear it. She sat back on the floor by the tub and listened anxiously.

In what seemed to her to be an amazingly short amount of time, Greg was pounding on the door and bellowing with rage when he found it locked. 'Sara! Dammit, Sara, unlock this door!' She jumped with shock at the loud booming sound the hammering at the door produced. He must have taken the stairs two at a time to get up here so fast. 'Sara, if you don't get over to this door and unlock it right this minute, I'm going to break it down!' He paused a moment, and after thinking it over, she thought the prudent thing to do would be to open the door. She inched carefully over as his voice changed and became suddenly very anxious. 'Sara? Can you hear me? Are you all right?—Oh, thank God!' That was as she clicked the lock open and turned the knob.

His expression of relief, however, soon turned to anger, and he took her by the shoulder to shake her hard. 'You stupid, selfish, idiotic—why the hell did you do that when you know you aren't strong enough to take a shower safely on your own? What if you'd got dizzy and fell? What if you'd hit your head in the shower and drowned before I could get to you? Of all the imbecilic things to do, this really——'

Infuriatingly easy tears spilled over on to her cheeks at this rough handling of her body. She was still sore in her muscles from the fever, and so very weak that her knees buckled up on her and she slid to the floor again, right out of his grasp. She crouched on the floor, crying, and Greg suddenly knelt down beside her to try and take her in his arms.

At this, though, she turned on him and spat with fury, 'How *dare* you touch me like that! How dare you lecture to me! Just who gives you the right, mister? Who the hell died and left you almighty God of the universe? Don't you think I'm capable of a rational decision on my own? I've managed pretty well for twenty-eight years without you, and haven't died yet! Kindly credit me with a modicum of sense, sir, and look around you. I'm taking a bath, not a stupid shower, and I can manage quite well without your help!'

Her voice rang out over the sound of gushing water, and she was shaking with the extent of her own outrage and fury. Still, one part of her mind bemoaned her loss of temper as she watched Greg's face grow rigid at her words. He looked like hard grey granite, but she looked into his eyes and saw a molten hot rage. He spoke quietly in contrast to her agitated outburst, and it was somehow more frightening than anything her anger could produce. The words came from between clenched teeth. 'I suggest, madam, that before you start rejecting help out of hand, you may wait until some is offered to you. I had no intention of doing so.' With that, he stood and left the room as swiftly as he had entered it.

Shaken, tired, depressed beyond words, Sara crouched for some time afterwards on the floor, crying her eyes out.

It was an ordeal to take a bath, but she managed it by going slowly and resting often. She even managed to soap her hair clean, though there was no pleasure in it any more. Then, sitting on the bathroom stool, she carefully towelled herself dry and cursed her shaking hands. She didn't want to be weak. She couldn't afford to be weak. She was on her own, like she had always been before. She had to handle things alone.

She barely glanced at the mirror as she carefully walked by. She had put on her housecoat and wrapped her hair up in a towel. Even so, the pale, huge-eyed apparition, a ghostly caricature of herself that had been reflected, made her pull up with shock. Her cheekbones were sharp and protruding, and her jawline more pronounced. She had noticed in the bathtub that she had lost weight, and it showed in her face. She looked at herself unemotionally before going on to the bedroom. After that first shock, it didn't really matter to her what she looked like. In fact, she didn't really care about anything. She longed to sleep.

Her wet hair had to be taken care of, though, and she plugged the hand dryer in a socket in front of the full-length mirror, sinking with trembling limbs on to the floor in front of it. Then she just sat there and looked at herself dispiritedly, wondering how she was going to get up the strength to hold her hands above her head for any length of time. A flicked glance at the doorway had her stiffening defensively. Greg stood watching her, his face inscrutable, impassive, serious.

Sara switched on the dryer with shaking hands and began to hold it to her wet hair. He just stood watching for a while, then the dryer was plucked from her hands and he was pulling up the chair that had been by the bed. She stared, yearning, aching for something, some word or touch, but what she said instead was, 'I'll do it on my own, thank you,' and the words sounded cold.

His response came tiredly, 'Don't be a fool, Sara. Give me the brush, will you?' Hardly realising what she was doing, she slowly handed him the brush. He turned the warm blowing air on to her head and began to rhythmically brush the thick strands out to aid the process. It was hypnotising, relaxing, comforting, and he was very gentle, teasing out the snarls so carefully, she never felt any pain. At first she sat with her slender shoulders stiff and her face wooden, but she was so tired, and the continued motion of his hands felt so good that she gradually sank down until her cheek rested on his knee.

A drop of wetness fell on his slacks and soaked into the material, then another followed. If Greg noticed, he never said a thing, and Sara soon stopped crying. Really, this was a very weak habit to get into, this crying all the time, she thought. I've cried more in the past week or two than I've cried in years. It will have to stop. It's got out of hand.

She knew why it had got out of control. It had happened at the same time her emotions had gone out of control. It had happened when she had met Greg, had become involved with a total stranger. It happened every time a barrier came up between them, for one reason or another. It happened every time he walled himself off from her.

Right now, he seemed a hundred thousand miles away. He was helping her and being very good and gentle about it, too, but his eyes in the mirror looked to be withdrawn. It made his ministrations even more bittersweet and painful. She resented that look terribly. It told her that he was somewhere else, but it didn't tell her where, and she was too tired to go after him. She didn't have the strength to reach out. All she could do was lay her head against his knee, dumbly accepting his moving hands, while her heart bled all over the floor. She was the loneliest person in the world.

She was also wrapped up so tightly in her own miserable emotions that the realisation that he had switched off the hair-dryer and was now only brushing her hair came over her very gradually. She became aware of the fact that her hair was totally dry, but he continued to brush and smooth it off her forehead anyway. She wondered if he was so far away that he didn't even realise that her hair was dry. It felt too good, though, for her to open her mouth and spoil it, so she kept silent and very still.

The conviction that he was far away in his thoughts left her totally unprepared for his sudden movement. The shock of him scooping her up in his arms to lift her on to his lap held her still for a moment. He just held her, cradled her, and rocked very slightly back and forth. It was so exactly what she needed that she melted completely, put her arms around his neck and buried her face against him. It hurt so, and yet seemed to be the balm her bruised self needed.

They sat this way for a very long time. Finally Greg stirred and picked her up firmly as he stood. His grip was so decisive, she didn't have any choice but to comply with it. The question of her objecting however, was academic. It never occurred to her. She was too tired, too passive, too much in need of whatever attention he would see fit to give her.

He carried her over to the bed and gently laid her down on it. 'You need a clean nightgown, don't you?' he asked her softly, and she nodded, glancing at the widening gap of her dressing gown. He disappeared and came back with a filmy garment held in one hand, and he insisted on helping her with it, which was all for the good, since she didn't know if she could manage on her own. Then he sat down on the bed, stroked with an absent hand the side of her cheek, and stared frowningly into her eyes. 'We have to talk.'

Her throat was dry and she had to clear it before anything would even come out. 'I know.'

'Would you like to wait until you're feeling stronger?' His consideration, after the explosive clash they had just recently had, jarred her up. She nodded, lips drawn tight to keep them from trembling. 'All right. Are you tired now, or would you like for me to help you downstairs?'

'If you don't mind,' she whispered, sounding terribly humble. 'I think I'll take a nap now—I'm tired.'

'Call me when you wake up. I'll be back with supper later on in the evening.' He stood and turned to go, and she rolled over in the bed to stare dumbly at the wall until she did finally go to sleep.

He was up later, like he had promised her, and he shook her shoulder gently to wake her up. She sat, rubbing her eyes, and took in the loaded tray hungrily. Greg sat and kept her company, though they didn't say much. It would all be said later. For the moment, they just existed together in silence.

When bedtime came, much later, Greg came into the room and took his black robe and started to head out the door. Sara watched him with apprehensive eyes, and called out before he could get far. He turned around to her with an obvious reluctance.

'Are . . . you coming to bed soon?' she asked him quietly. It was the only way she could think to frame the question in her mind.

He looked down at the robe held in his hands, the posture throwing his eyes into shadow so that she couldn't read the expression in them. 'I thought I'd sleep in the other room tonight.'

She felt shattered. 'Greg, did you sleep with me when I was sick? I remember you being there.'

He didn't look up. 'Yes.'

Her voice trembled with the effort of asking the question. 'Then would you please tell me why you aren't sleeping in here tonight?'

He did look up at that with a searching, questioning glance, and his answer came slowly. 'I thought it would be best if we were apart until we had a chance to—talk things out.'

It would be disastrous, she sensed intuitively, if they did that. He was retreating behind the wall. It was his instinctive escape to isolation. If he slept away tonight, then any hope of a future together would be destroyed. A sense of desperation came over her, and it gave her the courage to blurt out, 'Please—I want you to stay.' She couldn't say anything after that, because that said it all, and she watched him with pleading eyes.

She saw him close his eyes and swallow hard. Then he was flinging the robe on to the chair and coming towards her, shedding his clothes and climbing into the bed. A muscled arm flexed, reached and turned the bedside lamp off. He pulled her into his arms and curved his long body to fit into the curve of hers. Warmth and relief swept over her, and she was able to relax enough to get sleepy.

She suddenly whispered into the darkness, 'Greg?'

His answering whisper was immediate. 'What?'

'I'm sorry I yelled at you this afternoon. I have a nasty temper, I know, and I didn't mean what I said.' Her body tensed; it was suddenly very important for him to realise that before she let herself sleep.

'Hush, Sara. I'm sorry, too. Relax and go to sleep, sweetheart, we'll talk later.' That was all he said as he hugged her convulsively against his chest, then relaxed his hold again, but it was enough. The tension seemed to ease up and they were both soon asleep.

# CHAPTER NINE

By unspoken mutual consent, they kept to light matters when they conversed the next day. Sara recognised what they both were doing: they were both giving each other breathing space. They touched each other often, as if they had to convince each other of something, of what she couldn't say. She was full of nameless fears, for she sensed something despairing in Greg's attitude, something desperate in his eyes, though his face was calm and serene enough.

She couldn't shake the feeling that the world was going to end, everything was just going to fall apart, and on the surface life seemed just fine. It made her want to scream in terror, and all she did was smile at Greg in response.

That evening, they both sat in front of the fireplace and sipped cups of coffee. The supper meal had been almost totally silent and, for Sara, very uncomfortable. She searched for things to say, and came up with nothing. The silence wasn't the kind of companionable quiet that comes from a peaceful feeling or a long-standing relationship. It was the tense-filled silence that preludes something violent, a tropical storm, a wild destroying tornado, death. Sara shook herself hard at this and deliberately thought of something else.

Greg's face flickered with the flickering light thrown from the flames. His dark eyes caught the colour and reflected it. It seemed as if he had two tiny twin flames of his own, deep inside. His face revealed nothing to her; it rarely did. That was a good trick he had learned as a criminal lawyer, she thought grimly, that ability to hide one's emotions behind a face of granite stone. She wanted to slap it off his face, to shout, to plead, to go and crawl into a corner and lick her wounds like a hurt animal. She wanted to walk out the door without a second look back, uncaring and without regret. She sipped her coffee instead.

When her own voice sounded in the quiet, so still room, she jumped with surprise as much as Greg did. 'Please,' she said quietly. 'I know there's something on your mind that's bothering you. Could we talk now?'

He regarded her from under lowered brows, then nodded heavily. Still, he didn't speak for some time, and when he did, she spilled some of her coffee from the shock of his words. 'I was married once,' he admitted harshly. Sara automatically reached for a napkin to mop up the hot drops sprinkled on the floor.

'How long ago?' she asked him simply. It was indicative of the stern control she had to exercise over herself. She had nearly reached over to hit him. Why hadn't he told her before? Why the hell hadn't he waited for her? The irrationality of that thought made her smile to herself, wryly. What a fool she was over him!

'About eight years ago,' he replied, his voice flat and unemotional. The very passionless tone of his voice was terrible to hear. 'I was very young, twenty-four. She was a year younger, just twenty-three.'

'You find it hard to talk about,' she said. It was a statement, not a question, and he nodded without surprise at her perceptiveness. 'What happened?'

'She was a beautiful little thing, and spoiled rotten, but of course I didn't see that at first. All I saw were those big brown eyes and the golden mane of hair, and that naïve sincere way she had of saying things. It was three years of hell,' he said, and he might have been talking about the weather. Sara winced, and his eyes caught the look. He stared right at her and let her see the bitterness he was fighting to control with every word. 'Her father was rich, and he gave her everything she wanted. What I couldn't afford to give her, whatever she had her heart set on, she would run to Daddy for. And there were other men. I didn't find that out for about two years, though she'd been no virgin when I married her. And by that time I frankly didn't care. Infatuation is a rotten basis for a serious relationship, and mine had died some time back.'

A log snapped in the fireplace, and fell through the grating to the hearth floor, shooting sparks high up the chimney. Beowulf was stretched out at her feet, and she left the corner of the couch that she had been curled up on, to go down beside him and pet his sleek side. He lifted his head, looked at her briefly, and plopped his head heavily down on her lap. Greg poured her more coffee. It could have been a cosy scene, and looked it. Advertisement material, she thought ruefully.

'You'd have had to have been a student in law school, right?' The gentle prodding worked, and he shook himself out of whatever reverie he had fallen into to continue.

'I was just finishing up, and starting my career with a brilliant bang. Andrea loved to complain of how I neglected her for my studies and career. It was her favourite line to her father, and of course, when I confronted her with the fact that I knew of her extra-marital affairs. It sounded terrific; those big brown eyes were so guileless and hurt, and the small mouth quivered with just the right touch. I laughed at her!' Greg smiled a truly amused smile at the memory. 'It was my best revenge for any emotional hurt she might have inflicted on me. She just stopped and stared as if she couldn't believe her eyes. I don't think anyone had ever laughed at her before.'

On impulse, Sara reached out her hand, and he took it immediately to hold it hard. She had the funniest impression; she suspected that his disclosures were hurting her more than they were hurting him. She suspected that he was way ahead of her on many counts.

He was continuing. 'The night Andrea died, I issued her an ultimatum. We had a few people staying for the weekend, and she'd sent off signals to one of our single guests all evening long. It was too much—right in front of me, and with a fellow I liked and respected. I couldn't let her ruin him with her particular brand of mucky immorality,' the peculiar emphasis he was giving to each word made their meaning lash out with the sharpness of a whip, 'so after our guests had gone up to bed, we had a confrontation downstairs. I told her that she could either stop her extra-maritial activities and stay with me, or she could pack her bags and go, but either way I really didn't give a damn. She was just furious! She spat poison at me for about an hour or so, I really don't remember, then she went upstairs to pack. By that time we were doing fairly well financially, not as well as Andrea was used to, but we were able to afford a housekeeper and some daily help. It was the only thing that saved me later on, our housekeeper being up late in the kitchen and cleaning up things from that night's dinner party.'

Sara got a sudden chill down her back at his words, and when he paused, she whispered through dry lips, 'W-what do you mean, "saved"? What peculiar wording—were you in some physical danger, Greg?'

'Not really. I was having a drink after Andrea had left the den, and when she screamed and fell down the stairs, Mrs Owens, the housekeeper, and I both ran out into the downstairs hallway at the same time. Because of the floor plan of the house, there was no way that I could have pushed her down the stairs and have been back to the den in the few seconds it took us to react. To this day, I don't know if Andrea, poor bitch, had deliberately fallen down the stairs for attention and miscalculated the distance, or if she really did slip and succumb to an impulse of malicious mischief afterwards. I don't think she really thought she would die. She just opened up those big brown eyes and stared up at me, with everyone crowding around, and said, "Why did you do it, Greg? Why?" And then she conveniently and dramatically died. You look like you could use a drink.' This last was said dryly.

Sara's eyes were saucers at his extraordinary disclosures, and she whispered, 'I think I could, please.' His mouth twisted, but he went to fix her one, pouring a stiff brandy for himself. Then he settled back on the couch, after giving her the glass.

'Andrea's father raised all hell. To make a long, sordid story as short as possible, the press treated the matter like bloodthirsty hounds, snapping up the titbits that her father threw at them. The story was sensational news at the time. I don't suppose you read about it?'

She numbly shook her head. 'I was in California. I might not have noticed, anyway, even if the story had been circulated out there, but I don't think it would have got that far West.' He was telling her something devastatingly important, she knew that, but as yet she hadn't grasped the implications of everything he was trying to say.

'I lost my job with the law firm from the pressure Andrea's father was exerting,' he said quietly. 'I lost several "friends" over the whole affair, and most important of all, I lost my privacy. I don't want to tell you about that. I had to move in an effort to regain some measure of peace. Eventually, everything culminated into a trial. It was my first shot at both the defence and being the defendant, and it was a most illuminating experience. I never went back to prosecution again. I could never live with myself if, by any chance, I'd put an innocent person through that particular kind of hell.

'Eventually I was acquitted through lack of evidence,

which was quite relieving.' At that dry statement, Sara gripped her glass so hard, she feared it might break from the pressure. 'Mrs Owen's testimony was my sole defence—that, and the fact that a few of the guests remembered me approaching her body from the downstairs hall, not from the top of the stairs. And of course, during the court proceedings, all the sordid details of her extra-marital flings were dragged out into the open and duly noted for the sensation-seeking public.' His succinct wording, coupled with the concerned look she threw him, revealed to her just how badly he was hurt by the whole nightmare. She had been right, after all. Greg had gone through hell, and he was still bleeding from the wounds. His supremely bitter glance glittered at her, and he asked her mockingly, 'Does it bother you, Sara, to know that I might possibly be a murderer?'

Her own eyes widened with shock at that, and she stared at him speechlessly a few moments before answering. He really was worried what she thought of him! That repelling look was back in his eyes, she saw, and a hard mask clamped down on his features, and she was suddenly sure that it was fear that made him look that way. She sipped from her glass and asked him, deliberately casual, 'Greg, would you answer an irrelevant question for me?'

'If I can.' His face never altered or softened, and his body was held tense as though he expected a blow.

'Did you tell me a true story a few nights ago, about when you put putty in all of your neighbour's locks?' She stared into the fire calmly as she waited for his reply, sensing the puzzled glance he threw at her.

'Yes, I did.' He fell silent, waiting.

She turned her head and smiled at him serenely. 'You never killed your wife, Greg. Nobody with that fine a sense of conscience so young could. Were you really worried that I might think you did? Shame on you!'

She felt his body relax slightly, but not totally, and she suddenly knew that everything was not over yet. 'I thought perhaps you might,' he admitted carefully, 'but that wasn't all I was worried about.' He paused slightly, and she knew an inexplicable fear. 'I hope to God,' he finished quietly, 'that I never see another reporter again in my life.'

The words were a physical blow to her. She had just begun to see all of what Greg was trying to say to her, but she still didn't guess it all. She still wasn't quite to the whole truth.

'Greg,' she whispered, through stiff lips. It was time to tell him who she really was. He had the right to know, after all he had just confessed to her. 'Greg, I have something I need to confess, too, and—and I don't know how to say it.' She stopped and looked at him, her mouth dry, lips shaking. She couldn't go on. He would hate her for not telling him before. He would hate what she was.

He sat there, passively waiting. His face was gravely attentive, but his eyes were raw. 'The best way to say it is the simplest, Sara.'

'Oh, Greg!' she said, and it was a cry of pain. 'My professional name is Sara Bertelli, and I'm as public as you can get, I'm in the news, I'm always under exposure, I—I sign autographs, dammit, and . . .'

'I know,' he said quietly.

Of all the terrible revelations that night, this one hit her the hardest. She closed her eyes tight and doubled up, whispering, 'Oh, my God! When did you figure it out?'

Greg brooded into his brandy glass before answering. 'I couldn't figure out why you looked so familiar to me at first. When I saw the piano in your house and noticed how peculiarly cautious you were being, it all clicked into place. I have most of your records, and your face is on the majority of the covers.'

He had known. That was why he had acted so strangely that night; he had known all along. Her knees were raised, and she leaned her forehead on them so that he couldn't see the tears sliding down her cheeks. 'I tried to tell you several times, but the longer I didn't, the harder it was to confess. I—wanted you not to know, Greg, I'm sorry. I thought you hadn't recognised me.'

'Oh, Sara, you dear little fool,' he sighed, stroking her hair. 'How could I not, with that face and body? You underrate yourself, my dear. I would have seen it sooner or later. In fact, I was determined not to see you again, but I had to come back that night, and the fact that I couldn't stay away made me deeply angry, and I ended up taking it out on you. I went home cursing myself, sure that the next time I saw you I would tell you goodbye, and there you were, sobbing on my doorstep, so small and frightened and vulnerable. I couldn't walk away!'

'I love you,' she choked out desperately. 'I love you!'

'And I you,' he responded immediately, roughly, laying his head down on her shoulder. 'You gave me more in that one night of loving than Andrea did in three long years. Sara, I won't face the cheap publicity and invasion of my privacy again. Not after what had happened five years ago.'

She began to realise the direction his speech was taking, for the first time that night picking up the implications of what Greg was communicating, and she tried frantically to hide from the rest of his words by covering up her ears with her hands. But he was relentless, and he came down to kneel beside her, forcing down her hands so that she had to hear what he was saying.

'I love you, Sara, and it's really love for the first time in my life. You mean so much to me; you're so many different things rolled up into one delightful person!

You're beautiful, and you're funny, and deeply thoughtful. You're sensitive and fragile, and frighteningly vulnerable. You're kind, and compassionate, and you're a terrible invalid, but I love even that aspect of you! I want to marry you,' he said harshly, pain etched in every feature. 'I want that wild vitality that you pour into your music, I want your body beside me every night. I can't live your kind of life, Sara!'

She was shaking her head from side to side, in protest at what he was saying to her, and his hands tightened on her shoulders with the urgency of his speech, shaking her to make her acknowledge what she was hearing. 'No!' she cried. 'There can be compromises, Greg, and things worked out——'

He went right on speaking, over her protests, as if he didn't hear a word of what she was saying to him. 'You're going to have to make a choice! You can't have both me and your career.'

'Don't say it, Greg!' she sobbed, struggling to get out of his hold and away from his terrible ultimatum. 'For God's sake, don't ask it of me! I can't *take* this, damn you——'

He shook her harder. 'You've got to listen, Sara! You've got to pick one or the other, there's no other way. I'm sorry.' Then he let her go, as if he had only just realised what he had been doing to her, and she stumbled to her feet.

'I can't take any more tonight, I just can't!' she said brokenly, backing sharply away from him as he stood to tower above her. 'Don't touch me! I don't want you to get near me, do you hear? I—oh, hell, I have to get out of here!' And with that, she grabbed the afghan off the back of the couch and dashed for the back door.

He came after her. 'Please don't go out there—it's cold, and you've been sick. Will you just listen to me a minute, Sara? Don't——'

She slammed the door on his words and ran out into

the night. A chill wind touched her exposed neck, and she shivered violently, wrapping the afghan around her tightly for warmth. Then she headed down the path to the beach, unhappiness dogging her footsteps and confusion preying on her mind.

The feeling that she was being torn in two came back to her, stronger and more anguishing than before. She must have had a premonition, that night in California. She must have suspected something of this nature happening.

She felt like she was in shock, deadened throughout her limbs. She had sustained too many blows that night, had absorbed too much vital information. Her emotions were tangled and raw, and her thoughts too agitated. Greg had offered her something she had thought she wanted more than anything else in the world, but at such a painful price. She couldn't think about it.

The night was illuminated with a pale moonlight glow that was at once subtle and yet piercing clean, keenly cutting through the senses. Sara could see quite clearly. The shadows were bigger at night and more black, and the colouring was very surrealistic. Everything ranged from a pearly shade of ivory to dark violets and midnight blue. She picked her way delicately down to the beach and looked out on the shimmery sands in the pale light. The water was fairly calm, lapping gently against the shore. It looked peaceful. Just letting her gaze wander out over the huge lake induced a feeling of calm and peace. It was what she had needed so badly. It was a refuge, for a while.

She huddled into the blanket and settled herself on the sand, staring blindly out. The entire conversation from that evening was played and replayed in her mind, like a broken recording and a repetitive, jumping phonograph needle.

Everything made sense now; every inexplicable

response of Greg's, every puzzling inflection in his voice, every hidden motive. Of course he was wary of strangers! Who wouldn't be, after what he had been through? The wonder of it was that he had allowed himself to get close to her in the first place.

That was the one thing that she had sensed in Greg, that he had in common with herself: loneliness. He had been just as compelled towards her as she had been to him. Isolated so completely like he had been, it was only natural, a totally human response. Two lonely people finding kindred spirits in each other, but was it really love that he felt for her? Could he just be reacting against all the self-imposed isolation of the last five years? She couldn't know for sure.

She felt such racking torment, two such completely opposite desires. One half of her wanted to reach out with both hands and grasp at whatever Greg was willing to give her, and the other half yearned for the life that she had so briefly left. She could never go back to the crippling ambition in her previous life, but could she give up something that was so tied to the essence of her personality? How could she give it up?

The minutes slowly trickled into hours, and the hours slowly washed away the night. Sara never moved. She was never aware of the dark shadow that came periodically to the edge of the beach to stand silently, tensely, watchful and unobtrusive. She had almost forgotten Greg, incredible as it seemed later to her. She was wrapped up totally in her self.

It was the hardest and longest night of her life. Not even the eve of her mother's death had been as bad as this was to her. Eternity weighed on her like a stifling burden. Time meant nothing to her, and the passage of the night was merely an unimportant occurrence. She was, however, genuinely shocked when she looked out over the quiet water and found that she was able to see the far-off lake horizon. She turned exhausted, sleep-blurred eyes in astonishment to the east, and found the grey lightening of the pre-dawn creeping over the dark treeline. A sense of panic invaded her. She had pleaded for time from Greg, and he had let her go.

She had been on the beach all night.

It was time to go back, and time to decide. She couldn't waste any more time prolonging the inevitable. She had known her own response to Greg's ultimatum when he had issued it, had known and had run away from the pain of the choice, and had stayed away the entire night. She couldn't let him go through any more pain, couldn't put him through the agony of the wait any longer.

Feeling a hundred years old, she rose stiffly to her feet and shook out the sandy blanket, slowly making her way back to the house. It was a long, lonely journey all by herself, just as the passage of the night had been. She was so tired, the battle with her emotions taking her past the point of exhaustion. All she wanted to do was to go and lay her head on Greg's strong, broad shoulder and cry out her uncertainties and weaknesses and let his strength carry the burden of her choice.

She reached the door and put out a shaking hand to grasp the knob. It turned easily, and she pushed it open and went in.

# CHAPTER TEN

GREG was leaning against the counter, his shoulders hunched over a stale cup of coffee, and he was staring down into it, his hair tousled and his face grey and haggard. The quiet torment in his eyes as he turned to look at her made her nearly cry out. His night had been a slow torture too, and from the looks of things, he hadn't slept a wink.

There was coffee made, and things strewn about the counter, the coffee can open. It looked as if it was one of several pots made, and Sara dropped the blanket to go over and pour herself some. The liquid tasted much too strong, and was very hot, and she sipped it gratefully. The warmth seeped slowly through her insides.

She turned and found Greg watching her silently. Her slight smile was involuntary and sympathetic. 'It's hell, isn't it?' she murmured, her tired eyes staring down into the warm black depths of her own mug. 'Letting down your guard to finally care for someone—it's hell! Greg, I shouldn't have run out on you last night like I did, and put you through all of this worry and waiting. I'm sorry. I knew when I went out that door what my answer had to be to your ultimatum, but I just didn't have the courage to face it.'

He put down his cup slowly, his dark gaze on her face. She couldn't meet his eyes, but she knew he was looking at her anyway. The intensity of it burned her like fire.

'Do you know why I flew back to California?' she asked him, laughing a little shakily at the irony of life. He shook his head, his silence prompting her answer. 'I

178

went to sign a new contract to do a prime time television special. Isn't that rich? The coverage and the publicity would be tremendous. I could get out of the contract. It would just about break me financially—and I do have quite a bit of money, you know, plus the future royalties from the album that's to be released in a months' time. It would just about take everything in a lawsuit, and it would ruin my reputation as a professional, to break that contract. I could do it, though. It would be a clean, irrevocable break, because no one would come near me with anything remotely resembling a business contract again. It would be just like you want, I'm sure.' Her eyes finally lifted to meet his, and they were so stony, so full of hurt and bitterness, that he flinched from the sight.

'You know, don't you?' she continued, in that deadly quiet voice. 'You knew from the beginning that I couldn't do it, you knew when you laid down those terms. Is that why you made such a demand, Greg? Is that why you put me through so much pain? You made your demands so completely impossible for me, so that the responsibility for us breaking up would be wholly mine, didn't you?'

'No!' he bit out harshly, his face so lined with pain that she nearly broke down at the sight of it. 'I am what I am, Sara. You can't change what I am, even if you'd like to! It was a choice that you had to make—between me and your career!'

'That's a damned lie!' she burst out raggedly. 'Will you just listen to yourself a minute? Did you really hear what you just said? You've got it all backwards, mister. You haven't always been this way. You've let yourself become so embittered by your bad experiences, you've let this great big wall grow up around you. It's got so big, you can't even get close to anyone any more! You've made this whole relationship so impossible because of it, you—Greg, didn't we have something

good? Couldn't you like what we had? We—we shared.'
Tears blurred her vision, and she turned away from him
abruptly so that he wouldn't see, but of course he did,
and with an animalistic sound of pain he jerked
forward to pull her into his arms. She turned and clung
to him for a moment, and their lips met in a fierce,
intense, despairing way, then she was struggling to get
out of his arms as though he was about to choke her to
death.

'Sara, reconsider, will you——' he began hoarsely,
but she whirled on him in such a fury that he stepped
back from the intensity of the blast.

'My God!' she raged. 'Don't you dare ask me again,
Greg Pierson! You still don't have any idea of what
you've done to me, do you? You really don't know! Do
you want me to tell you just how badly you've hurt me?
You've become something so isolated, so alien and
inhuman, so incredibly unkind——'

'That's enough!' he barked out savagely, but she was
too enraged to heed him.

'Not by a long shot, it isn't!' she shot back swiftly.
'Look at me, for God's sake, just look at me! Do you
know what I am? I'm a singer! I'm a performer! I live to
make music for other people, dammit! You want me to
tear that out of myself, to give it up completely, never
to look back? Greg, it's not a job for me, it's my whole
life! You're asking me to cripple myself to accommodate
your inhibitions, and I—just—can't! Oh, I don't need to
tell you that I was sorely tempted. I want you so badly,
it—it tears at my insides. I wanted to reach out and
take what you're offering me, but it would all be a lie.
How long would we last together, do you think? How
long of the good before I would get to be resentful and
restless? How long before the fighting would start? How
long before my love would turn to hate?' She swallowed
painfully, grasping her trembling hands in front of her.
'I think I hate you already, for even asking it of me!'

Greg had turned his back to her while she was speaking, and it was symbolic of his entire life. She stared at the broad expanse with a look that was indeed almost hatred; she could see the wall in front of her, coming between them, cutting her in half and killing whatever they had once had. He was rigid, and he looked uncompromising. She felt the utter hopelessness of what she was trying to impart to him, and the bitterness of defeat. He would never come out from behind his wall. It had fused itself irrevocably to his personality.

'I almost said yes to you,' she said quietly, her voice hoarse from tiredness and pain, and his back grew even more rigid. 'But then it occurred to me, Greg, that you couldn't really love me after all and still ask that of me, and it was all so much more of a lie than I'd ever realised,' her voice shook horribly, and she saw his shoulders jerk. 'Some day, some day you're going to wake up and realise what you're doing to yourself, and do you know what's going to happen? That wall will have grown so much by then, and be so monstrously huge, that you'll never be able to get out again, no matter how you try. You're going to die of starvation, just waste away from lack of human companionship and understanding, and no one will ever know.' She hesitated and waited for some kind of response, but he was as if he were dead, so still did he stand, and she turned away to the open doorway that led out to the hall. 'Goodbye, Greg.'

She didn't see his face, for he was turned away from her, and so she was unaware of the silent tears that streamed down his granite-hard face, of the lips that were drawn back tight over teeth clenched with pain. She hadn't seen his fists, drawn down by his sides, and didn't know that his knuckles were white and the fingers bloodless from the tension of his tight grip. She was in the hall after saying goodbye, and the words he mouthed were a bare thread of sound anyway, so she wasn't to know that he whispered hopelessly, 'Don't go. Sara, don't go. Sara!' But he didn't call after her, and she trudged upstairs with a heavy heart.

Her clothes went into her suitcase with an agonising quickness. She kept hoping against hope that she would hear a sound at her open door and turn to see Greg there, accepting her for what she was, loving and supportive of her needs. The house was so unbearably silent. She knew that Greg would not come up those stairs. She rather suspected that he was already too far gone behind that barrier of his. It all was so hopeless.

She would have given her life for him. If he had been in trouble, or in danger, she would have gladly given her life. She simply could not forsake herself, though, give up her whole nature for him, or anyone else. Relationships, she reflected sadly, are a lot like alcoholism. You get addicted to a person, and no relationship is going to be pure pleasure or pure pain, and that's why it's so hard to leave. It's when the pain outweighs the pleasure that you have to go, and the pain of leaving is the hardest of all.

Divorce has got to be the ugliest word in the English language.

She had all her things together, and she went downstairs with her suitcases in hand. It felt like a betrayal, which was hard to justify. If she stayed, she betrayed herself, and if she went she betrayed her love.

The house was a tomb. Greg had apparently gone out, for which she was thankful; she didn't know what she would do if she had to face him again. A sudden feeling of panic came over her, and she stowed her luggage away swiftly in the trunk of her car. She felt the need to get out before she destroyed herself with her own need. She backed the car out of the garage, shut it, and was soon driving back to her own cabin. Her footsteps echoed eerily when she entered the front door, and she knew that for her own sanity's sake she couldn't stay long. A phone call to the airport secured her a flight in the afternoon, and she made other calls concerning her car being shipped back, careless of the cost and anxious only to get out of Michigan and as far away from Greg as she could.

It was perhaps revealing of her state of mind to know that she had called in her plane reservation as Sara Bertelli. That alone was a statement and an affirmation of her own self.

With a few hours on her hands, she went and stood in the bathroom to look at herself in the mirror. It had been a very painful vacation. Her huge and tired eyes stared at herself thoughtfully. She had come away from her work to find out who she really was, and had fallen in love. She had found herself, but at such an emotional cost. She knew her core, and it was the loneliest knowledge in the world, for she had no one to share herself with. It could have been wonderful with Greg. It could have been a celebration of her self and an adoration of his self, and it had all gone awry.

But she did know herself, and she was no longer ashamed. Going quickly out to the car, she hauled out her suitcase and handbag and re-entered the cabin to closet herself in the bathroom.

Some time later, a slim, vibrantly beautiful woman with hauntingly sad eyes came out. She was very chic and well dressed, and her hair was coiled intricately at the nape of her graceful neck. Her make-up was skilful and eye-catching, and her bearing distinctive.

Just as she was preparing to leave, the phone began to ring, and she stopped with a suddenness that nearly cost her her balance. She stared at the phone as if it were an apparition from the underworld, and her lips formed Greg's name. She headed for it and nearly picked it up, but then she thought that if he really had something to say to her, he would be over in person.

She didn't really want to talk to anyone else.

The front door was locked quietly, closed against the interminable ringing of the phone inside. Sara let herself into her car and drove away without a backward glance.

She parked the car at the train station where it was to be loaded, and filled in all of the necessary forms while waiting for the taxi she had called. It soon arrived, and she climbed into the back while the driver loaded her things. He had stared at her in that familiar, don't-I-know-who-you-are look, and she had smiled at him wryly, knowing instantly what kind of car ride she was to have on the way to the airport.

Sure enough, the man asked her all sorts of eager questions, and she handled them all with a charm and a patience that he would remember for the rest of his life. She even signed an autograph addressed to his teenaged daughter, for which he couldn't thank her enough. He was completely captivated by her, but at the same time he had enough perception to wonder at the almost unbearable sadness in her lovely huge eyes and the lines of tiredness that marred what otherwise he would have considered a perfectly featured face.

Sara stared out of the car window and silently wondered, when will the world stop seeming so grey and dreary? An utterly devastating depression had settled over her mind, a combination of lack of sleep and the knowledge that every mile the taxi travelled, every mile the plane flew, was a mile farther away from Greg.

She would never see him again. The thought made her nearly cry, right in front of the cab driver. She would never look into the eyes of the man who meant more to her than anybody else. She would never know what it felt like to sleep in his arms again, to wake to his sweet smile, to hear his rich warm laughter.

She missed the beach already, and she missed Beowulf. Would the dog miss her? she wondered. The next natural thought faltered. Would Greg?

Maybe he was relieved to have her gone at last.

She eyed the parking lot of the airport with loathing. The trip would be hard, harder than the one coming back to Greg, when she had been so ill. The taxi driver was extremely accommodating, opening her door for her, like royalty, and carrying her luggage into the building. He was a really nice man, she thought, as he deposited her bags next to a luggage carrier with a flourish that could have been European. She gave him a handsome tip for his kindness, and he shook her hand vigorously in farewell. It was all very exhausting.

She had enough time for a meal at the airport's restaurant before the flight left, so she headed in that direction after taking care of her luggage. Everywhere she went, heads turned and whispers passed from mouth to ear excitedly. Was it really she? Dare we ask for an autograph? Sara was used to the attention and never even so much as turned a hair at the amount of notice she was attracting. There was an aura of reserve about her that kept people from coming up and asking for her autograph. Aside from the constant, wearing attention she received from a young giggly waitress, she was left strictly alone.

She toyed with her salad, eating only enough to keep herself from collapsing from hunger, and she sipped listlessly at her coffee. The brew was pretty terrible, and most of it was left to cool in the cup.

She wasted away the rest of the time she had left, and finally had to leave her comfortable seat in the restaurant to board her flight. For some reason the airport was crowded that day, and she had to push her way through people to step on to the escalator that would carry her to the second storey, where she would be boarding. Her heart ached.

Greg, she thought, and she could hear his voice calling her from outside her cabin, that day when he had brought all the firewood over to her place. A

pity she hadn't been able to stay and use it up. The
gesture had been nice. Her eyes flooded with moisture.
His voice had sounded deep and hoarse from anxiety.
'. . . Sara! Sara, listen to me! Can you hear me? Sara!'

She gradually became aware of someone really and
truly calling her name, and suddenly the world whirled
and her stomach lurched, and she had to grab for the
side belt for support as she turned to look out over the
crowd that she was rapidly rising above. She would
have sworn she had heard Greg's deep voice bellowing
out over the babble of the crowd.

Her eyes swept out over the people, and she shouted,
'Greg! Greg, is that you?' and then her eyes found him.
He was fighting to get through a thick patch of people,
his dark face grim, and his eyes desperate. He found her
as she called out, and for a split second they stared at
each other as she was pulled farther up and away. She
yearned with all of her being to push past all the people
lower down on the escalator and throw herself at him,
but she just couldn't. The first move had to come from
him. He had to tell her.

Even at that distance, Greg must have been able to
read her need and uncertainties, for his head lifted and
he shouted out, 'Sara—Sara Bertelli, please don't go!'
She stared, absolutely stunned to the core, and heads
lifted at the famous name, faces turning towards her
and murmuring. 'Sara,' it was a roar of, incredibly,
exasperation, 'for God's sake, I love you!'

He couldn't really get more public than that.

She was at the top of the escalator without realising it
and tripping over the stationary boarder, as she stared at
Greg from the top of the stairs. She was immobile, frozen,
while she watched him struggle to get to the bottom of the
escalator. Someone came up to her and touched her arm,
saying, 'Gee, Miss Bertelli, I'd really love to have your
auto——' But the person was talking to empty air, for
she suddenly found the power of movement in her legs

and was racing to the down escalator, murmuring
apologies as she wriggled through people. Then she was
stumbling down the moving stairs and pushing by two
outraged old ladies, squeezing past a portly gentleman,
incredulous joy beating at her temples, pounding in her
veins. He saw her approach, and changed direction to
meet her at the bottom of the stairs.

Then everything seemed to be going in slow motion,
and everything was incredibly clear. Sara was able to
remember each movement and jostle and expression on
Greg's face for the rest of her life.

She reached the bottom of the escalator after an
eternity. He came forward between two people,
thrusting his broad shoulder aggressively through the
slight space between them and ignoring their protests.
His dark hair looked ruffled as if he had ran his fingers
through it repeatedly, and it glinted like newly minted
copper in the harsh fluorescent light. His face was at
once both haggard and harsh, with lines running from
his nose to the sides of his mouth and in between his
heavy brows, and yet at the same time his face was soft
and more open than she remembered it. His eyes blazed
with a fierce, radiant glow, expressive and vulnerable.
Then his two hands were reaching for her eagerly, as
eagerly as she was reaching for him, and they fell
together urgently.

Her face was pressed painfully into his jacket as he
strained her to him, nearly breaking her ribs. She didn't
mind; she wouldn't have cared if the roof came
crashing down around them; she would have smiled
sweetly if someone had come up and bashed her on the
head. Nothing mattered outside the press of his cheek
on her hair and the pressure of his arms around her.
She knew that she must be holding him as tightly and as
painfully as he was holding her, but all she saw when
she lifted her head to look into his eyes was a deep and
steady strong glow of happiness.

The murmurs around them and the fingers pointing didn't matter in the least. Sara couldn't care less, and she was immensely touched and amused to see Greg reacting with a supreme indifference as he tilted up her chin with an exquisite tenderness to bring his mouth down on hers in a gentle, giving, healing kiss that lasted just exactly for ever. She never heard the scattered applause about them; she was too wrapped up in the man holding her, and her own delirious happiness. She could have sworn that she had literally seen the smoking ruins that he had stepped over in order to reach her in liberation.

The wall had crumbled to rubble at last.

Excitement was tense within her, almost making her sick to her stomach, heightening her senses. Her eyes, made up skilfully and dramatically, were huge and brilliant, glittering and sparkling. They were the focus of her face. When one looked at her compelling features, the eyes always drew the gaze. Her black hair was styled into a profusion of glossy curls cascading all about her face and shoulders, and her skin-tight outfit was very, very black. It fitted like a body suit, cut low on the shoulders and encasing the legs, and was worn with a glittering silver overdress that was very transparent. Her silver high heels were dashing, sleek, emphasising her height. She waited in the wings, patiently submitting to the fussings of the make-up artist, the hairdresser, and the costume designer, but she paid no attention to any of these. She was alone, isolated, preserving the build-up of power and energy that would spill out of her in just a few moments.

People ran back and forth behind the stage curtain. Directions were called out quietly, positions were being taken. The special was being filmed live, and the months of work and creative output and musical effort were coming to their culmination tonight. Sara listened to the audience out in front with her breathing shallow and her luminous eyes slightly dilated. It was almost exactly like a live concert, the difference being that millions of people would be seeing her perform instead of mere thousands. She was as tense as a live wire.

The celebrity guests were close by, being prepared just as she was, but she paid them no mind either. All of her being was focussed on herself, her hypnotic state of preparation. Nothing could go wrong, she knew that instinctively, with that inexplicable, intuitive realisation that sometimes comes to an artist.

It was almost time. Her heart thudded, roared, pounded. Her hands shook and her lips compressed. She was sick, she was fine, she was like a thoroughbred horse quivering and intent on the starting gate opening up to the most gruelling and important and vital race of her life. A few more seconds only, just a few more, then she would be going out on that stage, moving in front of so many people, in front of so many ... her head turned slowly, her eyes sought out the darkness backstage, and she caught sight of the tall silent man who stood in a small oasis of stillness in the frantic movements around him. His eyes were on her and her only, fixated, concentrated. They just looked at each other for a long moment when their gazes locked. Her own were fierce, slightly mocking, strangely pleading and compelling under delicate black winged brows. Greg's were dark, intent, searching and approving. He nodded to her slightly, once, and it was all that she had needed. It dispelled the doubts and fears of the past few months in one careless sweep. He understood, she realised finally, he really understood.

Then the curtain was raising and she was grabbing the microphone and stepping strongly out on to the stage, her movements lithe, eager. The music pounded out a heady beat, quick, tense, lilting. The crowd caught sight of her moving, glittering, arresting figure and roared, clapped, screamed. The energy that she had tremblingly held in for the past few days burst forth in the dynamic and riveting melody of her song. She had to hold the microphone down a bit, a little bit away from her lips and slender throat, for the musical sound coming from her was overwhelming and powerful, elemental and earth-shattering. She could have dropped the microphone altogether and sung loud enough to fill the entire auditorium, the power pulsed so in her veins. Her body moved gracefully to the sounds, compellingly; people could not tear their gaze away. The crowd drank her energy up, just soaked it in like a sponge, and that was okay because she had more to give inside of her.

Later, after the show, she would go with the dark silent man and they would put in a token appearance at the party being held in her honour, and they would go proudly, side by side. Then she would go home with him, and he would bring her down to earth, get her back in touch with a sane reality, hold her when she crashed from the energy high that she was feeding from at the moment. She would probably be so tense and excited still that they would make violent love, and then they would sleep peacefully together, in each other's loving arms, exhausted. She wanted to go home with him, wanted to have that give-and-take relationship with the man who would always be a bit of a loner in the eyes of the world. She wanted to race along the beach with a black panting loyal beast, and lie quietly in the arms of the one who loved her best for every single facet of her complex personality.

But that was the completion and contentment of another part of her. And that was to be later. For now Sara was giving to people her best gift of music, and only she and one other knew that it was given mostly to him. She was pouring out everything in her full and intensely happy heart, sweat coming out on tense neck muscles and collarbone and gleaming in the white hot spotlights. She was performing the music of her soul.

It was the fulfilment of her destiny.